Birthday Pie Burial

The Drunken Pie Café Cozy Mysteries, Book Two

By Diana DuMont

Chapter One

Edgar Bates was the most energetic one hundred year old you'd ever see—and as we neared the fourth hour of his birthday celebration, he seemed to only get more energetic. While many people who were decades younger than him were starting to show signs of weariness, Edgar was still talking and laughing loudly, telling anyone who would listen about the great birthday speech he planned to give.

I heard everything he said from my vantage point behind the dessert table, where I'd been stationed to make sure that only adults ate my boozy pies. I owned the Drunken Pie Café in downtown Sunshine Springs, where I served both alcoholic and nonalcoholic pies. For Edgar's grand one hundredth birthday celebration, the mayor had asked me to provide a smorgasbord of both types of pies. I had happily obliged, and my pies had been one of the more popular desserts at the party. Right now, all that remained was apple bourbon pie, rhubarb rum pie, and one slice of lemon vodka pie.

My Dalmatian, Sprinkles, sat at my feet in a huff. I knew he'd been hoping for a slice of pie at the end of the celebration, but I refused to feed him alcoholic pie. Since all the nonalcoholic pies were gone, Sprinkles wasn't going to be getting any treats tonight. I reached down to scratch him affectionately behind his spotted ears.

"Don't worry, boy. I'll be sure to save you a nice big slice of pie from the café tomorrow." Sprinkles barely raised his eyes to look at me. He wasn't appeased by this promise, but there wasn't much I could do to cheer him up at the moment. I couldn't magically make another pie appear out of thin air.

"Sunshine Springs has never heard a speech like the one I'm going to give them," Edgar suddenly bellowed at the top of his lungs, drawing my attention away from Sprinkles. Edgar waved his right hand in the air wildly at the same time that I swatted away the right hand of a teenage boy who was trying to steal the last slice of lemon vodka pie.

The boy made a face at me just as Peter Bates, Edgar's son, made a face at his father.

"Okay, dad. Come on. Everyone gets it. You're America's next great orator. But we don't have time for your rambling speech at the moment. The fireworks show is about to start, and you don't want to miss the fireworks being set off in your honor, do you?"

Peter pushed Edgar's wheelchair toward the front of the large, grassy lawn. Many people had already spread out picnic blankets to sit on while they watched the upcoming fireworks show, and Edgar greeted them loudly as Peter pushed him along. Beside me, my best friend Molly laughed.

"Looks like Peter is the party pooper at his dad's own hundredth birthday party," Molly observed.

"Not surprising," a deep male voice said from behind me.

I spun around to see that Sheriff Mitchell McCoy, known to everyone in Sunshine Springs simply as Mitch, had arrived at the dessert table. He gave Sprinkles a good rub behind the ears, then grabbed a plate and loaded it with two slices of rhubarb rum pie.

"Why is it not surprising?" I asked. "Is Peter not a big fan of his dad?"

Mitch smirked. "Not really. Not since his dad started dating a thirty-year-old blonde bombshell."

Molly spit out the sip of lemonade she'd just taken. "Edgar is dating a thirty-year-old? That's a seventy year difference! She could be his great-granddaughter!"

Mitch shrugged. "Well, look at you, Molly. You've got some good math skills."

I rolled my eyes at Mitch as Molly punched him soundly in the upper arm.

"I'll tell you who has good math skills," I said. "Edgar's thirty-year-old blonde bombshell. I'm sure she's run the numbers and realized that squeezing her way into Edgar's will is sure to bring a huge increase to her bank account balance."

Mitch pointed a finger at me and winked. "Bingo. And Peter isn't too bad at math, either. He realizes that every dollar his father

3

leaves to Tabitha instead of him is one less dollar in his own bank account once his father's will is probated."

Mitch swallowed a huge bite of pie, and I wondered how he managed to stay so fit and muscular when he was always eating so much junk. Every time I saw him he was either downing one of my sugary, boozy pies, or he was stuffing his face with chocolate croissants from the Morning Brew Café, another Sunshine Springs hotspot.

"Speaking of blonde bombshells," Molly said. "I'm assuming this must be Edgar's new flame heading toward us right now."

I followed Molly's gaze and saw a tall, skinny blonde with a Barbie-sized chest heading toward us. The woman teetered precariously in a pair of sky-high heels, and I wondered how many little holes those heels had put in the grassy lawn she'd just come from.

"Yup," Mitch said, chewing around another bite of pie. "That's Tabitha alright. Tabitha Miller. Just the woman Edgar was waiting for over the last hundred years."

Tabitha approached the dessert table, wringing her hands anxiously. "Thank goodness Peter is finally gone. I've been wanting to come by here and get some booze, but I can't stand to be within fifty feet of that horrid man."

She glanced down at the slice of lemon vodka pie. "Do you have any straight up vodka? I'm sure your pies are delicious, but I really just want the vodka. Adding pie to my liquor only adds unnecessary calories."

Beside me, I heard Mitch snort with laughter. I gave him a good, hard kick in the shin, and smiled politely back at Tabitha.

"I'm sorry. I only have boozy pies, not straight up booze. You might want to head over to the Sunshine Springs Winery table. Theo has a large sampling of his best wines, and they're completely separate from any sugary pie."

I glanced over at the Sunshine Springs Winery table, and Theo Russo, the winery's owner, caught my eye. He grinned at me and waved. I waved back, admiring the way his tanned skin glowed in the soft light of the streetlamp positioned right above his table. I wondered for the umpteenth time whether I had been a fool to decline Theo when he asked me to come to this party as his date.

I'd told him that I wasn't ready for a new relationship, and that was true. I'd just been through a nasty divorce, and my heart needed time to heal. But looking at him now, I had the strange, panicky feeling that some other woman was going to snatch him up before I had the chance to take him up on his offer to date me.

A loud sigh from Tabitha brought me back to the present moment. "Never mind, then. I'll just skip all of the calories altogether. Edgar has some excellent whiskey back at the house. I'll just drink some of that when this party is finally over and I can go home. For now, I'm going to go hide out in the bathroom and freshen up my makeup."

Molly frowned. "But the fireworks show is about to start. You'll miss it."

Tabitha waved her hand in annoyance, as though swatting away a persistent fly. "I can't stand fireworks. They're so loud, and what's so exciting about a bunch of explosions in the sky? I really don't understand why anyone over the age of ten would waste time watching that nonsense."

She sauntered off toward the bathroom in a huff, and I arched an eyebrow as I watched her go. "Looks like Peter isn't the only party pooper."

"Speak of the devil," Mitch said. I looked up to see that Peter was walking back toward the dessert table at a rapid pace. He was now wearing a bright orange baseball cap that made him look like he was setting off for work at a construction zone. I resisted the urge to roll my eyes. He looked ridiculous in that hat.

My own grandmother was a fan of bright neon outfits, but she pulled them off much better than Peter did. I'd seen Grams earlier in the evening, and had dutifully admired her hot pink shift dress. A month ago, that dress would have matched her neon pink hair. But Grams had recently changed her hair color from hot pink to lime green. I was sure that within the next month it would change again. Perhaps to electric purple?

"I think I finally got my old man to settle down for a bit," Peter said as he grabbed the slice of lemon vodka pie that Tabitha had declined just a minute ago. He took a huge bite and chewed for a moment, shaking his head in annoyance as he did. "I keep telling Dad that no one wants to hear an old man rant, but he's insisting on giving his speech once the fireworks are done."

Beside me, Molly shrugged. "Give the old man a break," she said. "If anyone deserves a chance to rant, it's someone who's made it to their hundredth birthday party. Odds are good that your father won't have many more opportunities to rant in his lifetime."

Peter scowled. "Fine by me. Trust me, if you have to listen to him rant later, you'll understand why I've been trying to convince him not to give a speech."

Peter shoved the other half of the pie into his mouth. Then, in a voice muffled by all that pie, he mumbled something about going to check that everything was in order for the fireworks display.

I shook my head in disgust as he rushed off. "Honestly, I don't blame Edgar if he writes Peter out of the will. You'd think that his own son would be a little more accommodating of him at his hundredth birthday party."

"You'd think," Mitch said as he wiped the last crumbs of pie from his face. "But it's not that surprising, really. Peter has always been a bit sour toward his dad, and it's gotten worse as time goes on. Peter used to at least make an attempt to act polite, but a couple years ago when Peter's business really took off and he made his own fortune, he started treating his father with more and more disrespect. Now that Peter is wealthy in his own right, I guess he doesn't feel quite as much pressure to avoid being written out of his father's will. Of course, that doesn't stop him from complaining incessantly about Tabitha and how she's trying to swoop in and steal the family fortune."

"What a mess," Molly mused.

But before any of us could say anything else, another Sunshine Springs resident was approaching the dessert table. I recognized Belinda Simmons as one of the employees down at the Morning Brew Café. When she was selling chocolate croissants, Belinda always had a big smile on her face. But right now, she looked quite unhappy.

"Is everything all right?" I asked.

She glanced over her shoulder nervously before looking back at me with a strained expression on her face.

"Yes, yes," she said hurriedly. "Everything's fine. I just need to go check on something quickly."

Before anyone could say anything else to her, she ran off into the shadows.

"What's the matter with her?" Molly asked.

"She probably got in another fight with her husband," Mitch said. "Every time I've seen Frank and her together lately, they're at each other's throats. It's sad, really. They've been married for twenty years, and have always seemed so happy together until now. Hopefully they work out whatever issue they have going on."

I didn't say anything. After the awful divorce I'd just gone through, I didn't exactly feel hopeful when I heard about people struggling in their marriages. Thankfully, the first round of fireworks started just then, and I didn't feel the need to say anything else. Molly, Mitch and I turned our gazes toward the sky, and watched as brilliant shades of red, blue, orange and green lit up the darkness.

The city had really gone all out in organizing this party for its oldest citizen. The fireworks show we were watching rivaled the best Independence Day fireworks I'd ever seen. Out across the grassy lawn, the rest of Sunshine Springs' citizens seemed just as enthralled. Everyone's heads were turned upward toward the sky as the brilliant display continued. When the grand finale finally came, I felt my heart swell with pride. I felt so lucky to be part of this town. When I first moved here from San Francisco, I hadn't been sure that the locals would ever accept me as one of their own. Grams had promised me that it would just take time, and I should have trusted her. She'd lived in Sunshine Springs her whole life, so she knew the people well. Still, I'd worried. But she'd been right. Now, I truly felt at home in this close-knit community.

As the finale ended, a moment of quiet passed over the expansive, grassy lawn. When it was clear that the show was really done, cheers started going up. At the front of the crowd, I saw Edgar struggling to stand out of his wheelchair. He raised his hands high and clapped, clearly pleased with the fireworks that had been set off in his honor.

Suddenly, one more loud boom rang across the field. I looked up at the sky, expecting one last firework. But the only light in the sky now came from the stars and the crescent moon. Confused, I lowered my gaze.

And then, I heard another sound: screaming.

Loud cries of "He's been shot! He's been shot!" rang across the field. Everything seemed to erupt into sudden chaos. People were standing up from their picnic blankets and running. Some ran away from the front of the crowd, and some ran toward the front. I looked at where Edgar had been, hoping that someone was helping him in the midst of the commotion. But I couldn't see him any longer. His wheelchair still sat there, but it looked empty. Where was he? Surely, he wasn't trying to run all by himself?

I looked around, expecting to see him hobbling off the field without assistance. He was just spunky enough to attempt to take off on his own in the midst of an emergency instead of waiting for help from Tabitha, Peter or someone else nearby. Not that Tabitha or Peter were nearby at the moment. Tabitha was still hiding out in the bathroom as far as I knew, and I hadn't seen Peter come back from checking with the pyrotechnics about the fireworks show.

"Oh, no!" Mitch suddenly said beside me. Then he took off running toward the field, yelling. "Police! Police! Out of the way!"

As the crowd parted to make way for him, I saw that he was heading toward a crumpled heap of a man that was lying next to Edgar's wheelchair—a crumpled heap of a man that looked exactly like Edgar.

Chapter Two

Without thinking, I started running after Mitch. Sprinkles followed right on my heels, barking excitedly as he ran.

"Izzy! Wait!" Molly called from behind me.

I barely heard her. A sick feeling of dread was growing in my stomach. The glimpse of Edgar I had seen through the crowd had not looked promising. I wasn't sure what I could do to help, but I had to at least try to do something.

When I arrived at the front of the field, Mitch was already there. So was Theo. He must have run over from the winery's table as soon as he heard the screaming start. Right now, Theo was bent over Edgar's body, trying to perform CPR. To my surprise, I saw that Theo had tears in his eyes.

"Come on, buddy!" Theo said between attempts to re-inflate Edgar's lungs. "Come on! Just hang on until the paramedics get here!"

But it was no use. The pool of red blood underneath Edgar's body grew larger by the second. Eventually, Mitch gently reached down to pull Theo back.

"It's no use," Mitch said. "He's gone."

The paramedics were rushing up, but Mitch was right. Edgar had died at his own hundredth birthday party. I clasped my hands over my mouth in shock. The sight of all that blood was making me a bit woozy, and I didn't understand what had just happened.

All around me, people were screaming. Several people were saying something about a gunshot, but my mind refused to comprehend the words. To my relief, I caught a flash of lime green off to my left. Grams was running up to me, and I held onto her arm like she was a life raft and I was drowning in a churning ocean.

"Are you alright, Izzy?" Grams asked me.

"Yes," I stammered out. "But I don't think Edgar is."

Grams shook her head sadly, her lime green bob bouncing from the movement. "No," she said as we both stared down at Edgar's body, which was now surrounded by paramedics. "I think Edgar is far from alright."

All around us, people were crying and screaming. Mitch was trying to calm them down, and was yelling at everyone to stand back. But no one seemed to be listening to him. Everyone was in a state of shock.

And that shock only increased when one of the paramedics looked up and shook his head. "Dead on arrival. He's a goner."

Gasps ran out across the crowd, followed by both angry screams and horrified sobs. I clung to Grams' arm for dear life, and beside me, Molly came up and clung to my arm.

"I don't believe it," Molly said, staring down at Edgar's lifeless form.

Theo came and stood beside us, too, shaking his head in shock. More Sunshine Springs police officers had arrived on the scene, and were trying to push back the crowds.

"Everyone back!" they yelled. "This is a crime scene! Everyone back!"

Slowly, the police managed to clear a space around Edgar. I wanted to look away, but I couldn't. My brain wouldn't let me stop staring until I understood what had happened.

As though he knew how confused I was, Theo started to explain. "He was shot. When he stood at the end of the fireworks show to applaud, someone shot him."

The sick feeling in my stomach started growing larger once again. "But who would do that? Who would shoot an old man at his hundredth birthday party?"

Just then, an almost inhuman scream pierced through the night. When I looked in the direction of the scream, I saw Tabitha running through the crowd, hobbling horribly as she tried not to fall over on those ridiculous heels she was wearing.

"Edgar! My Edgar!" she wailed. When she reached the body, she threw herself down across it, not seeming to notice as the dark blood stained her pale pink dress. I hated to be so cynical, but I wondered if she was really feeling grief at that moment, or if she was putting on a show. If Edgar had written her into the will, I was sure people would question how real her relationship had been with her lover who was seventy years her senior.

But real or not, Tabitha wasn't the only one putting on a display of grief. Another horrified shout rang out across the lawn, and I looked over to see Peter running toward the scene.

"Dad!" he yelled. "Dad, no! No, no, no!"

Peter threw himself toward the body as well, conveniently pushing Tabitha backward as he did.

"Don't push me away!" she yelled hysterically. "He loved me more than you, and you know it!"

"You're crazy!" Peter snarled. "I'm his only son! You're just a lowlife gold digger who was trying to swindle him out of his fortune."

"Both of you need to step back!" Mitch roared over the noise. "This is a crime scene, and you're contaminating it!"

Peter and Tabitha continued to yell at each other, even as several police officers stepped in to pull them away from Edgar's body. I finally looked away.

"Come on," I said to Molly. "Let's clean up the dessert table so we can get out of here. This party has turned into a disaster."

Grams and Molly followed me as I made my way back toward the dessert table. Grams kept shaking her head and clucking her tongue, asking over and over who would do this.

Molly and I remained silent. I didn't know who could possibly be horrible enough to shoot a one hundred-year-old man, but it hadn't escaped my notice that Peter and Tabitha had both been gone from the field during the fireworks show.

Peter hadn't seemed too happy with his father, but would he actually shoot him? And Tabitha likely stood to gain from Edgar's death, but would she have risked losing her chance at Edgar's fortune by murdering him? She didn't seem to be the most intelligent person I'd ever met, but she'd have to be really dumb to murder a man who was going to probably die soon, anyway.

None of this made sense, but I didn't think that standing around listening to the town's citizens discussing it in hushed tones was going to help me make any more sense out of it tonight. I just wanted to clean up my portion of the dessert table and get out of there. I hurriedly started stacking the empty pie dishes, and within minutes I was ready to go. I bid Molly and Grams good night, promising to see them soon. They seemed just as eager as I was to get going.

But Sprinkles hesitated and whined softly as I turned toward the parking lot. I turned back toward him.

"What is it, boy? There's nothing left to do here. We should get home."

He whined again, and I looked in the direction he was looking. I felt an uneasy feeling pass through me as I saw a lone figure running through the shadows—a lone figure that looked like Belinda Simmons. Why was she slinking away like that? That seemed awfully suspicious, but I pushed the worry out of my mind. Belinda might have been acting strangely lately, but I couldn't see any reason she would be connected to Edgar's murder. What motive would she have had to kill off the old man?

Still, I figured I should try to mention it to Mitch tomorrow. He would want to know about anything suspicious that had happened at the party, and he would definitely want me to tell him what I'd seen instead of trying to chase down Belinda myself. Mitch didn't like it when I tried to play detective. Not that that had stopped me before, but I was trying to do a better job of minding my own business.

"Come on, Sprinkles," I said. "Time to get out of here before we get any more tangled up in this mess."

Chapter Three

As expected, the murder of Edgar Bates was all anyone talked about the next day. I was determined not to get involved in this case, but it was hard to turn a deaf ear when every single person who came into my pie shop was discussing it. Even the tourists were talking about it. Tourist season was slowly winding down, but we still had quite a few people coming through from the big city, a.k.a. San Francisco—and even the tourists had heard about the shocking shooting of Sunshine Springs' oldest resident.

Those tourists all asked me what I knew about the situation, and I tried to tell them I didn't know anything. But inevitably one of the locals would pipe up and insist that I did.

"But surely, Izzy, you must know something," they'd say. "You were right there when it happened, after all. I saw you standing next to Edgar's body."

I tried to explain that I hadn't exactly been right there when it happened. I had actually been quite far away when the gunshot went off. But I had run up quickly to the scene of the crime, so everyone thought I had been there when Edgar toppled over.

I didn't know any more than the next guy, and that was fine with me. Not too long ago, I had been involved in solving another murder here in Sunshine Springs. That had been enough for me. I had no desire to become a regular sleuth, but apparently, people in Sunshine Springs didn't forget things easily. All the locals kept reminding me that I was a good detective, and asking me what I thought of this case.

What I thought of this case was that it was pretty obvious who the most likely murderer was. As far as I knew, the only people in town who hadn't been on the grass or at the nearby food tables when the gunshot went off were Peter, Tabitha, and possibly Belinda.

Belinda had no motive to kill an old man, and I couldn't imagine that Peter would want to kill his own father—especially if he was currently not sure whether he was listed in the will or not. Most likely, he would have wanted to wait until his father's little fling with Tabitha wore off before seeing his father die.

That left Tabitha as the most likely suspect. While she didn't exactly strike me as the type who would know how to use a gun, who was to say that she wasn't just acting like a dumb blonde to fool everyone? Perhaps she had gotten nervous and wanted to make sure Edgar died while still in love with her. That way, her bank balance would benefit from her time suffering as the girlfriend of a one hundred-year-old man.

And, honestly, could it really have been anything other than suffering? Even after my nasty divorce, I wasn't one to begrudge someone true love. But I didn't know anyone who would take a relationship between a one hundred-year-old and a thirty-year-old seriously. It must have been a bit torturous for Tabitha. But I guess people could endure quite a bit when large sums of money were at stake.

I wasn't alone in my suspicions of Tabitha. Most of the people who came to the café that day were also pointing fingers at her. Molly, who was helping me out at the café because I hadn't been able to hire another employee yet, was working with me that day. Her normal job was to work as the head librarian of the Sunshine Springs Library, but she took on shifts at the Drunken Pie Café both to help me out and to earn extra money to pay off her debts faster. I was glad she was here today. She helped me fend off many of the nosy gossips who kept trying to pull me into conversations about Edgar.

Molly agreed with me and everyone else that all signs pointed to Tabitha as the killer. I wondered what Mitch thought of everything, but I wasn't about to call and ask him. I knew if I made any mention of the murder to him, all I would get was a stern lecture that I needed to stay out of it and let him take care of the police work. I was still considering mentioning to Mitch that I'd seen Belinda acting strangely, but the more I thought about it, the more ridiculous I felt for suspecting her. She had probably been acting strangely because she was in a bad mood over a fight she'd had with her husband, and Mitch would only laugh at me if I suggested that he needed to investigate her.

Of course, calling Mitch wasn't the only way to figure out what Mitch thought. When the bell above my café door jingled and I looked up to see Scott Hughes walking in, my heart leapt. Scott worked as a delivery guy in Sunshine Springs. Chances were good that if you needed a package delivered, he was going to be the one delivering it. That meant that Scott spent all day going around town to different homes and businesses. He was one of the best sources for gossip in this town, and, thankfully, he was my good friend. I knew that if he'd heard anything about the case, including what Mitch thought, he would let me know.

Judging from the smile on his face as he made his way up to the front counter with a large box in his arms, I had a feeling that he had plenty to tell me.

"Good afternoon, ladies," Scott said to Molly and me. "I don't actually have a package for you today, but I thought I'd act like I did so that I could come say hello."

I rolled my eyes at him. "You know, you can just come say hello, right? You don't have to act like you have a delivery. You could just act like you want some pie."

Scott grinned. "That wouldn't be acting. I always want pie. Got anything good today?"

"Here. Try a slice of this mulled wine crumble. It's a new recipe I'm trying out to get ready for my fall menu, and I think it's going to be a keeper. I'm almost sold out of it and we're still a few hours away from closing time."

"I'd be happy to test it and give you my honest opinion," Scott said magnanimously. He grabbed a fork and set the box down on the counter so that he could wolf down the mulled wine crumble.

Molly glanced over from the cash register where she had just finished ringing up a customer. "Hey, no free dessert!" she said. "If you want pie, then you have to pay for it with the latest gossip news."

I grinned at Molly, and then nodded at Scott. "My thoughts exactly."

"I'm getting to that," Scott said around a mouthful of pie. "This is delicious. Possibly my favorite yet, although I must admit it's hard to beat out the death by chocolate pie."

"Enough with the pie discussions," Molly said impatiently. "Hurry up and tell us what you know about Edgar before more customers come in. We've barely had a break all day, and we have one now. So spit out what you know and be quick about it."

"Alright, alright. Calm down," Scott said. "I don't think what I know about Mitch's suspect list will be that much of a surprise to you. Tabitha is the number one person of suspicion, of course. She probably stood to gain the most from Edgar's death, and she wasn't present by his side when he was shot. It stands to reason that she might have been hiding somewhere with a gun, ready to take Edgar out. Peter is being interviewed as well. He wasn't with his father at the time of the shooting, and presumably he might get some money from the will. Of course, it seems much less likely that a son would kill his own father, but you never know. Peter had quite a temper, and he and his father fought often. In fact, many had seen them fighting the very day of the party."

"When we saw him he didn't seem too happy with his father," Molly said. "I wouldn't exactly say they were fighting, but Peter was having a fit that his father was insisting on reading a speech he'd prepared."

I nodded. "Yup. Edgar was insisting he would read it after the fireworks, and Peter was trying to convince him not to. But I guess in the end it didn't matter, since dead men can't read speeches."

"Right," Scott said. "Anyway, that's pretty much the extent of the suspect list right now. But the more interesting news is that I heard something about Edgar's will."

Molly and I both leaned in. This definitely sounded interesting. No one who had come through the café today had been able to offer any insight into what the will might say, but everyone wanted to know whether or not Peter had been written out in favor of Tabitha.

Scott lowered his voice and looked around to make sure no one was listening. The bell above the door jingled, and Molly and I both glanced up to see a new group of tourists coming in.

"Hurry up," Molly hissed to Scott. "Spit out what you know before I have to go wait on these customers. Who's named in the will?"

Scott shrugged. "I don't know who exactly is named in the will. That hasn't been made public yet. But what I did learn is that Edgar asked that his will be read in public. He apparently stipulated that anyone who wanted to listen should be allowed to hear the entire thing being read in Town Hall of Sunshine Springs."

I furrowed my brow. "Really? That guy did have a flair for the dramatic, didn't he? Who asks for their personal business to be read aloud to the entire town?"

"Edgar Bates, that's who," Scott said. "And don't act like you're not going to go to the reading."

"You're right," I said sheepishly. "Of course I'm going. I'm sure the whole town is going. We all love our gossip here in Sunshine Springs. As the town's oldest resident, Edgar knew that better than anyone. Maybe this was his last gift to the town—one last splash of gossip."

Scott chuckled. "Yup. Edgar knew that everyone in Sunshine Springs would be whispering about who would get his fortune after he died. I guess he wanted us to all be able to find out at once."

Molly rolled her eyes. "That's a bit ridiculous if you ask me."

"You think so?" Scott teased. "So you won't go to the reading, then?"

Molly made a face at him. "Of course I'm going to go. I love gossip as much as the next person in Sunshine Springs. Still, did he have to be so obvious about his need to be at the center of all the town's drama? Even in death he wanted to be in the gossip spotlight."

Scott just laughed. Molly had to go help the café's newest customers, who had now decided which kind of pie they wanted. I turned to Scott to ask him whether he'd heard anything else from Mitch, but the café's phone rang before I could get the words out.

I sighed. "Sorry, I need to get this. We've been crazy busy today. On top of the tourists that have come out for the nice weather, all the locals are trying to get in on a piece of the gossip."

"No worries," Scott said. "I've already told you everything I know, anyway. I'll let you know if I hear anything else. And thanks for the pie."

As Scott turned to head out of the café, I reached for the phone. I shouldn't complain about being busy, but I was annoyed that I'd had to cut my conversation with Scott short. Even though he'd said he hadn't heard anything else, I had still wanted to pick his brain about exactly what he might have heard down at the police station.

Oh well. There would be more time to talk with him later. Perhaps I could convince Molly and Scott to both come out for a drink with me this evening. It would be nice to hang around with two of my best friends for a bit, even if none of us had anything interesting to add to the gossip.

"Drunken Pie Café, Izzy speaking," I said into the phone.

"Oh, hello," said a woman's voice that sounded slightly familiar. "I was wondering if it was possible to get some pie delivered. I'm really hungry, but I don't exactly want to go out in public right now."

I frowned. "Sure, I can do a delivery. But it will have to be after we close at five. The store's too busy for me to leave right now. Would that be okay?"

The caller let out a long sigh. "I suppose that's okay, if that's all you can do."

"Great," I said, ignoring the sigh. I wasn't about to feel badly that this person would have to wait another hour or two. I was doing them a favor to even deliver at all. "What kind of pie would you like? And who is this?"

"I would really love a lemon vodka pie, if you have one. And this is Tabitha Miller."

I nearly dropped the phone. Tabitha wanted me to deliver pie?

Perhaps I was going to have some good gossip to share later on, after all.

Chapter Four

Less than thirty minutes later, I was on my way to the late Edgar Bates' house to bring Tabitha a lemon vodka pie. The Drunken Pie Café didn't close for another two hours, but when I told Molly who had called and what she wanted, Molly had insisted that I go right away to take Tabitha some pie. Molly had been afraid that if I waited too long, Tabitha would change her mind and order food from somewhere else. Neither Molly nor I wanted to take the chance that we might lose our opportunity to get some inside gossip.

No matter how much I tried to tell myself that I didn't want to be involved with another murder case, my curiosity was getting the best of me. And so, I found myself ringing the doorbell of the giant Bates house, hoping that Tabitha might say something interesting in the few minutes it took me to drop off the pie.

When Tabitha opened the door, I still hadn't figured out what I was going to say other than "Here's your pie." Frantically, I tried to think of something to say that would encourage her to talk. But I needn't have worried. It turned out that Tabitha was desperate to talk.

"Thank you so much for coming right away with the pie," she said. "I can't tell you how difficult this day has been. Would you mind terribly coming in for a few minutes? I feel like I'm going crazy in this big house by myself."

I wasn't about to pass that up. "I understand. I'd love to keep you company for a few minutes. This must all be so hard for you."

A look of relief flooded Tabitha's face. "Oh, you have no idea. It's been horrible. This morning there were several news reporters camped out in front of the house. Then later on there was a group of people with signs that read 'Murderer' chanting outside my door. Peter himself came by to let me know that he didn't appreciate the fact that I had killed his father. He tried to come in, but I wouldn't let him into the house. He said it was rightfully his now, but I told him that it wasn't unless the will gives it to him."

"You poor thing," I murmured as Tabitha led me into a spacious kitchen. I set the pie down on the kitchen's island, and Tabitha went to get two plates and a serving knife.

"Won't you have a piece with me?" she asked.

I was about to refuse, but, as if on cue, my stomach growled. I smiled sheepishly at her. "I guess I will. I haven't eaten anything all day because the pie shop has been so busy."

Tabitha cut me an extra large slice, and I dug in right away. Not only was I starving, but I was hoping that if I was too busy eating to talk that Tabitha might start talking. I wanted to hear everything she might be willing to share.

She didn't seem that talkative right away, though. She pushed little pieces of pie around on her plate with her fork, and sighed heavily more than once. I waited her out. I had a feeling that if I kept quiet long enough, she would eventually say something.

I was right. She finally looked up at me and blinked as though blinking away tears, but I noticed that there didn't seem to be any actual tears in her eyes.

"This has all been such a shock. I know that many people think I didn't love Edgar, but I truly did. I cherished every day we had together, and I truly wasn't after him just for his money."

I frowned. "But I'm sure you can see how it appears that way?"

Tabitha gave me a sharp look. "Think what you want to think."

I thought she was going to kick me out then, but she merely lapsed back into a sullen silence for a few minutes. I took another big bite of pie, not sure what to say to her. To my surprise, when she finally spoke again, she had suddenly changed her tune.

She threw her fork down, and threw her hands in the air in frustration. "Okay, fine. So maybe a little bit of my motivation for being with Edgar was the fact that he was filthy rich. Can you blame me for jumping on an opportunity to live such a comfortable lifestyle? Don't tell me you wouldn't do the same thing!"

She looked at me accusingly, and I shrugged noncommittally. To be honest, I wasn't sure what I would do if a hundred-year-old man who was filthy rich offered to date me. The idea of dating someone so much older than me seemed repulsive. But at the same time, I couldn't predict what I would do if a virtual fortune landed in my lap with only the requirement that I pretend to be enamored with an old man.

Tabitha slammed her fist on the island once again, and I jumped. I dropped my fork on my plate and it clanged loudly, but Tabitha didn't seem to notice. She was looking past me now, her eyes staring unseeingly at the wall behind me.

"I know people think I'm just a dumb blonde," she said. "But I'm not that dumb. Why would I murder Edgar to get his fortune when he was on death's door as it was? I mean, come on. The dude was a hundred years old. All I had to do was wait a few more months—a year or two at the most—and he would no doubt have died of natural causes. Why would I risk going to jail for life myself and losing a potential fortune just to speed things up by such a small amount of time?"

She had a point. I wasn't sure I quite believed that she was innocent, but I decided to act like a sympathetic friend and see what else she might be able to tell me.

"You're absolutely right," I said in a voice that I hoped sounded deeply concerned. I even reached across the island and patted her hand sympathetically. "But of course, in a situation like this the police will always look to what seems like the most obvious suspect. Can you think of anyone else who might have had a reason to kill Edgar? Did he have any enemies that you know of?"

Tabitha shook her head slowly in frustration. "Not that I know of. Don't get me wrong. He did have people who didn't like him. His personality could be, shall we say, *abrasive*? He didn't really give a crap what anyone thought of him, and sometimes that meant that he was downright rude to people. I guess once you reach a hundred years of age, you don't feel like you have time to waste acting as if you like people that you don't actually like. You just say what's on your mind, and that's that. Unfortunately, that tends to rub people the wrong way. Edgar had definitely offended quite a few folks in Sunshine Springs, but I can't imagine that anyone would have killed him just because he was rude to them."

I couldn't imagine either. I had only met Edgar a handful of times, and he had undeniably been someone who didn't care what people thought of him. And yes, he was often a bit on the rude side.

But nothing he had said had been worth killing him over, at least not that I'd heard. Still, I pressed on. If Tabitha had not been the one to kill him as she claimed, then there had to be someone else out there in this town who had a reason to hate him.

"Are you sure there wasn't anybody he was on the outs with? Perhaps someone he had been so rude to for so long that they just couldn't take it anymore?"

Tabitha laughed bitterly. "No one except his son. If you ask me, I think Peter is the most likely suspect. He constantly fought with his dad, but he would always try to make up for it later. He didn't care about Edgar at all, but he was terrified of being written out of the will. Oh, Peter always claimed that he didn't need his dad's money because he himself was rich. And Peter *is* rich—I'll give him that. His business is wildly successful. But I suppose that no matter how much money one has, some people still want more. Peter is a greedy person. He fought with his dad, but not too much. He didn't want to lose his chance at getting a nice big inheritance and becoming even richer than he already is."

Tabitha rolled her eyes as she took a big bite of her pie. I resisted the urge to point out the fact that she could hardly blame Peter for trying to manipulate his father to get more money when she herself had been dating Edgar just to get his money. She didn't seem to notice or care about this apparent contradiction.

In fact, now that she had admitted to me that Edgar's money was basically what she was after, she seemed to feel free to unload her worries on me about whether she would be getting anything from his will. She put a huge bite of lemon vodka pie in her mouth, and didn't bother to finish chewing it before asking me if I'd heard about the public will reading.

I nodded. "I heard. It sounds like Edgar wanted everyone to know who his fortune was left to."

She nodded. "I'm worried. What if that means that he didn't leave me anything? Maybe he wanted to humiliate me in front of the whole town."

I chewed on my lower lip for a moment and considered this. "Why would he do that? It sounds like he truly cared about you, even if you maybe didn't care as strongly about him."

Tabitha shrugged listlessly. "Edgar was the sort of person who would get a laugh out of something like that. He would think it was hilarious to string me along and make me think that I was getting

22

money from him, and then humiliate me in front of the whole town by giving me nothing. I'm so nervous about this will reading. I don't even want to go, because I'm so afraid that I'm going to be horribly embarrassed. But if I don't go, it will look like I didn't care about him at all."

She shoved another bite of pie in her mouth, and I tried to think of what to say next. It sounded like she truly hadn't cared about Edgar that much at all, so why would she think that I would be sympathetic to her plight? I decided as I watched her chew her pie that she was probably one of the most selfish, self-absorbed people I'd ever met. The supposed love of her life had just died, and here she was eating pie and bemoaning the fact that she might be embarrassed.

She clearly wasn't in mourning at all. She was dressed just as fashionably as she had been last night, her hair was done neatly, and her makeup was flawless. Her eyes weren't red at all. I doubted she'd shed a single tear over Edgar. If she had cried any last night, it was probably only because of the stress of becoming a potential murder suspect.

I wondered again whether there was any truth to the accusations against her. Who could say? It was true that she didn't have much to gain by killing Edgar off early. But she did seem like the impatient type who was used to getting what she wanted when she wanted it. Maybe she'd decided that she didn't want to wait another year to become filthy rich.

Before the silence between us could get too awkward, we were both startled by a sudden crash coming from somewhere else in the house.

Tabitha looked up at me with fear in her eyes. "What was that?"

If I hadn't been a bit frightened myself, I probably would have made some sarcastic comment about how there was no way I would know what it was if she didn't. It was her house, after all. At least, it was the house she lived in at the moment. I guess no one would know whose house it actually was until after Edgar's will was read. But still, there was no reason for me to know what was causing the crashing noise any more than she did.

The noise sounded again, and Tabitha dropped her fork on the island with a clang.

"Someone's broken into the house!" she exclaimed.

Fear gripped my heart. If Tabitha wasn't the murderer, then someone else out there was. Were they trying to take her out, too? And was I going to be caught in the crossfire? I wanted to run and hide behind the large dining room table that stood nearby, but I told myself that panicking was only going to make things worse. I tried to put on a brave face.

"Maybe it's one of those crazy picketers with their 'Murderer' signs," I said. "They're probably just trying to harass you. I doubt it's anyone truly dangerous."

Tabitha didn't look convinced. "Why would they go to the trouble of actually breaking in? They don't care about Edgar that much, do they?"

Then a look of seeming understanding passed across her face. "Maybe someone thinks that they can break in and steal some of his valuables now that he's not around anymore."

I felt myself breathing a sigh of relief. She was probably right. Someone probably thought they could make off with something of value now that Edgar was dead. I wasn't about to die in the crossfire of a second murder after all.

But Tabitha wasn't relieved at this information. I saw her eyes darken with anger. "I'll show them! If they think they can steal from my inheritance, then they deserve what's coming to them!"

She ran full speed into the nearby living room and grabbed a giant poker from the fireplace. Then she ran toward the front entrance, where the sound had seemed to come from.

"Tabitha, wait!" I called after her. "Don't hurt someone! It's just stuff! Don't do something you'll regret. Even if someone took something, there are still plenty more valuables in this house, I'm sure. It's not worth killing over."

I winced as that last sentence came out of my mouth. There was a decent possibility that Tabitha had already killed over the stuff in this house. If she'd already murdered Edgar, what was to stop her from murdering someone who was trying to steal Edgar's stuff?

In any case, Tabitha was not interested in stopping. She reached the front room just as the front door swung open and then slammed shut. Someone had definitely been there just moments before.

"Stop, thief!" Tabitha yelled as she ran across the room. But she was wearing the same high heels as the night before, and she tripped over the edge of a rug in her wobbly haste. She screeched in pain as she went down, landing hard and sending the fire poker clattering across the room.

"Oh, no! Are you all right?" I tried to help her up, but she pushed me away and kicked off her high heels as she jumped to her feet again.

"I'm fine! Stop the thief!"

She ran toward the door, and I shrugged and followed her. When she threw open the door and looked around, I looked over her shoulder. At first, I didn't see anything. The large, well manicured front yard seemed empty. But then, a rustling in the trees by the northern border of the yard caught my eye.

"Over there!" I yelled. I watched as a shadowy figure disappeared into the trees with a flash of orange—the exact same shade of orange as the baseball cap Peter had been wearing the night before.

Tabitha swung her head around, but she was too late to see anything. The intruder, whether he was Peter or someone else, was gone.

Tabitha spun angrily around and marched back into the house.

"This is a disgrace!" she yelled. "I'm calling Mitch right now to report a burglary, and he'd better find that thief and stop them. He seems to have plenty of time to falsely accuse me of murder, so he needs to find time to stop thieves from taking over what's rightfully mine!"

I decided that it was a good time to make my exit. I thought Tabitha was acting ridiculous, and the longer I stayed the more tempted I would be to make a sarcastic comment about her actions. There was no point in making her angry.

Besides, if Mitch did come out to investigate the burglary, I didn't want to be here when he arrived. No matter how much I tried to explain why I was at Edgar Bates' house, I knew Mitch would think I was trying to take over his case.

I did have to admit that I found the case intriguing at this point. At the very least, I could hardly wait to see what the reading of the will would reveal.

Chapter Five

The next few days passed relatively uneventfully. I shared what I had learned with Scott and Molly, but after the initial excitement of discussing who might have broken in to Edgar Bates' house, our insights into the murder investigation seemed to come to a standstill.

Scott tried to get information from the police station when he made deliveries there, but Mitch was being as tightlipped as ever. The staff at the police station had all been ordered not to discuss the case, so Scott couldn't learn anything from them either.

I tried to shrug it all off like I didn't care. I told myself that the burglar had likely been Peter, and that, despite her insistence that she would not have actually pulled a gun on Edgar, Tabitha was still the most likely suspect. When it came down to it, this case wasn't really all that interesting. Mitch could have it to himself if he wanted.

At least, that's what I tried to tell myself. But I was a curious person, and no matter how much I acted like I wasn't wondering about the case, I had to admit that it kept popping up in my mind.

Luckily for me, Edgar's funeral was scheduled for the third day after he died. Peter said he wanted a simple affair, but Tabitha insisted on going all out with a huge celebration of Edgar's life. It was obvious to everyone in town that no matter what Peter wanted, Tabitha would automatically want the opposite. In the end, the funeral ended up being somewhere in the middle. It wasn't exactly the party of the century like the hundredth birthday party had been, but it was still a rather large affair. The whole town was invited, and of course the whole town decided to come. Even those who had not been that close to Edgar were not about to pass up the chance to be involved in the Edgar Bates saga in at least some small way.

I, of course, was no exception. When the doors to the local Baptist church opened on the morning of the funeral, I was right there along with everyone else in town, waiting for my chance to get in and be part of the action. I quickly found Molly, Scott, and Theo, and the four of us formed a little group as we headed into the church. We occupied a half a row not too far from the back. I didn't want to be too far from the exit.

Churches made me nervous. I had never been religious, so I only ever came to churches for weddings and funerals—neither of which seemed like particularly happy affairs to me. My own wedding had eventually resulted in a divorce, and funerals were sad for obvious reasons. I was glad I had been one of the first in line when the doors to the church opened, so that I could grab my safe spot in the back.

It didn't take long for the church to be completely packed. The place was standing room only, and while it would have been nice to think that this was because Edgar had been such a long-standing pillar of the community, everyone knew it was more because his death had come about in such a scandalous way.

As the last stragglers filed in, an organist played a somber hymn. I squirmed uncomfortably in my seat. I was wearing a dress and heels, and the stiff dress felt constricting. As for the heels, they were an incredibly rare occurrence for me. Even when I had been a lawyer, I had insisted on wearing flats to court. I couldn't stand heels, and reserved them mainly for funerals and weddings. I didn't know how Tabitha managed to walk around in them every day. Although, when I really thought about it, she didn't actually manage that well. The last time I'd seen her, she'd tripped horribly over her heels while attempting to catch the would-be burglar in Edgar Bates' house.

Tabitha herself was walking into the church at that very moment, and she was once again wearing heels. Today, her heels were black, but no one was fooled into thinking she had dressed somberly for the occasion. Those black heels were covered with shimmering rhinestones that looked more appropriate for a club than for a funeral. She had at least managed to wear a simple black dress that looked appropriate for a funeral.

As she walked down the middle aisle toward the front row seat that had been reserved for her, she noisily blew her nose on a handkerchief and sobbed. I wanted to roll my eyes. I was sure that this was all just a show she was putting on to make it appear like she had actually cared about Edgar and was truly heartbroken over his death. I looked over at Molly, who was sitting on the other side of Scott from me, and saw from the look on her face that she must have been thinking the same thing.

I wished that I had managed to sit directly next to Molly, but Scott and Theo had both shoved their way into a seat next to me. And while it was flattering to have two men vying for my attention, there were times when I really just wanted to be next to my best girlfriend. Right now was one of those times.

Not that I would have had long to be able to talk with Molly, anyway. The service was about to start, because a few moments after Tabitha, Peter entered the church. He wore a somber black suit that was completely appropriate for the occasion—no rhinestones to be found anywhere on his attire. He made his way calmly toward the front of the church with a resolute look on his face.

He didn't make eye contact with anyone, although several people tried to reach out and grab his arm to offer their condolences. I watched his behavior curiously. Was he acting so sullen because he didn't know how to deal with his grief? Or was he feeling guilt over having killed his own father? I decided it must be his grief.

Peter may not have been best friends with his father, but he had still taken at least a little bit of care with him. After all, on the night of the hundredth birthday party, he had been dutifully wheeling around his father's wheelchair. He'd been complaining nonstop about his father while doing it, true. But there was no law against complaining.

I wondered for at least the thousandth time that day whether Peter's halfhearted attempts to act like a good son would pay off. The will reading was scheduled for tomorrow afternoon. Would Peter be named in the will? Or would his attempts to maintain a relationship with his father have proven futile?

As Peter took his seat in the front row, the organist finally stopped playing. I heard the loud sound of knuckles cracking behind me, and I turned to see that Mitch was sitting there. Mitch grinned and gave me a small wave. I waved back before turning around to face the front again. Mitch had an annoying habit of constantly cracking his knuckles, and I always gave him a hard time about it. I think he did it on purpose to annoy me, even though he claimed it was just a bad habit. But there was no time to complain to Mitch right now. The church's pastor was standing and heading for the pulpit to begin the service.

But the fact that the service was starting wasn't enough to stop Peter and Tabitha from fighting. The pastor opened his mouth to begin, but before he got the first word out, a loud shriek came from the front row. Startled, I nearly jumped out of my seat. When I looked to where the shriek came from, I saw Tabitha had jumped to her feet. She was shaking a fist in Peter's direction.

Peter jumped to his feet as well, and before I could fully comprehend what was happening, I saw Tabitha's fists flying toward Peter's face. Gasps sounded out across the church as Peter lifted his hands to defend himself.

"You're a disgrace!" Tabitha yelled. "An absolute disgrace! How dare you?"

"I'm a disgrace?" Peter roared. "You're the one shamelessly trying to steal an old man's fortune by pretending you actually cared for him."

"I did care for him!" Tabitha shrieked.

Everyone in the church pews seemed to lean forward as one. We were all eager to see how this latest drama would play out.

The minister stood uncertainly at the pulpit. His hands were raised in midair, where they had been moments before as he had prepared to start his sermon. Now, he seemed to be wondering whether to stop and wait for this commotion to resolve itself, or whether to just continue on in the face of the mini-hurricane happening on the front row. I looked over at Molly again, and she looked back at me with wide eyes.

Scott couldn't hold back a chuckle. "Who needs theater tickets when you can just come see this mess for free?"

I gave him a dirty look. "Don't be so irreverent. This is a funeral, for crying out loud!"

"Don't lecture me about being irreverent," Scott said with a laugh. "I couldn't possibly be more irreverent than those two up front."

He was right, of course. I didn't think that things could get much more irreverent than a man's two potential heirs disrupting his funeral by yelling at each other while attempting to punch each other's lights out.

"That's enough!" a voice behind me called out.

I knew before I even turned around that it was Mitch. Still, I turned around to see. Mitch had risen from his seat to head toward the front of the church. As people in his row made way for him to get out, movement by the back door of the church caught my eye.

Belinda Simmons had entered the building. She stood uncertainly, watching the commotion unfolding before her. She must have decided that this circus wasn't worth her time, because she turned back around to leave the church.

But before she disappeared behind the heavy wooden doors, I caught a glimpse of a bright orange scarf peeking out from behind her conservative navy blazer.

Chapter Six

Even with Mitch's help, it took a good ten minutes to calm Tabitha and Peter down enough to be able to get the service started. When they finally settled, I couldn't stand it anymore. I had to sit next to Molly so that I could whisper to her during the service.

"Switch places with me," I whispered to Scott.

Scott happily obliged, since that meant he'd still be sitting by me but Theo wouldn't. Theo, on the other hand, wasn't too happy about the new situation, since he was no longer sitting next to me. He made a face at me, and leaned over to ask in a loud whisper, "What's the matter? Do I smell?"

I ignored Theo and turned my attention to Molly instead. Sometimes, Theo and Scott could really act like they weren't any more mature than two teenage boys. Scott felt like he had some sort of claim to me since he saw me more often than Theo, but Theo was used to getting what he wanted. Theo was wealthy, and had always had girls chasing after him. In fact, Molly had admitted to me that in high school she had spent her fair share of time pining after Theo. But, as so often happens when it comes to matters of the heart, the one girl Theo actually wanted was the one girl who wasn't interested in him right now: me.

I didn't care about Theo's ego. All I wanted right now was to talk to Molly. I hadn't mentioned to anyone yet that I'd seen Belinda sneaking off the night of the murder. Instead, I had convinced myself that there was nothing to it other than Belinda's own personal problems with her husband. But something about the way that Belinda had snuck in and out of the funeral made me think that perhaps my initial instinct had been right. Was Belinda somehow connected to Edgar's death?

"Did you see Belinda Simmons just now?" I asked Molly.

Molly looked back toward the door, but Belinda was long gone. "No, I didn't see her. Was she here?"

I nodded, and then in as quiet of a whisper as I could manage, I told Molly about how I'd seen Belinda sneaking off the night of the murder. Molly furrowed her brow as the organist began playing again. A woman with a very high soprano voice started singing a hymn in a screeching sort of way.

"Was Belinda really all that suspicious?" Molly asked. "I don't see how she would possibly be connected to Edgar. You're probably right in thinking that she was just sulking around the night of the party because of a fight with her husband. Mitch himself had just told us that they were fighting constantly."

Scott leaned over and tried to butt into our conversation. "What are you girls talking about? Don't leave me out of the loop."

I glared at him. "Hush. I'll tell you later."

Scott made a bit of a pouty face and sat back in his seat, while a woman in the row in front of us turned around and glared at me. I gave the woman a small smile. Really, I wanted to ask her what the big deal was. It's not like I could be any more disturbing or disrespectful than Tabitha and Peter had both already been. But I didn't want to waste time trying to explain that to someone who was already annoyed with me. Meanwhile, Theo glared over at all of us, still annoyed that he was no longer sitting next to me. I ignored him and turned back to whisper to Molly again.

"I thought at first that I was reading too much into Belinda's actions, but it bothers me that she showed up at this funeral looking just as sullen as she looked the night of the party. And why did she leave so suddenly? I think she knows something. Not only that, but I noticed she was wearing a bright orange scarf."

Molly shook her head, at a loss. "So?"

So," I said. "Don't you remember what I told you about the break-in that happened while I was visiting Tabitha? The burglar was wearing orange. I thought it was Peter with that stupid orange hat he likes to wear. But what if it was Belinda?"

Molly looked unconvinced. "Why would Belinda break into Edgar Bates' house?"

"I don't know," I admitted. "I'm just saying that she seems to be acting strangely. I think we should keep an eye on her."

Before Molly could say anything else, another commotion at the front of the room drew our attention. Tabitha had started to loudly complain about how incompetent Peter was. Peter was standing up once again and pointing a shaking finger in Tabitha's face.

"I'm not incompetent!" he yelled. "I'm just not myself these days because I'm grieving so much. You wouldn't know about that. You're not really grieving. You didn't really care about my father!"

The two of them started yelling at each other again, and Mitch, who was still sitting toward the front of the room after the last brawl, quickly stood to try to calm them.

I looked over at Scott. "What are they fighting about now?"

Scott frowned at me "Why should I tell you? You won't tell me what you and Molly were talking about."

"I will tell you, I just wanted to tell Molly first. I can't speak loudly enough in here to tell both of you at the same time or they're going to kick me out for disrupting the funeral."

Theo glanced over. "I don't think anyone has to worry about getting kicked out for disturbing anything. It would be hard to top those two."

"What are they fighting about?" I asked Theo.

Theo was glad to have information I wanted. He wasn't going to hold back the way Scott had. "One of Edgar's friends was supposed to read the speech Edgar had prepared to read at his hundredth birthday party. You know, the one he never got to read because he got shot first. But apparently the speech has been misplaced. Peter was supposed to bring a copy but didn't."

Now that Theo was offering information, Scott wasn't about to be outdone.

"Yeah," Scott interjected. "Peter is saying that he forgot the copy of the speech at home, and Tabitha is yelling at him that he's an incompetent fool and did it on purpose."

I turned my gaze back toward the front of the room. Mitch was unsuccessfully trying to separate Tabitha and Peter, who were only getting more worked up as time went on. Beside me, I saw Molly shake her head.

"It's a wonder Edgar didn't die of stress before being shot," she said. "Do you think they were always like this, or did Edgar's death make it worse?"

I shrugged. "Who knows? But the will reading is tomorrow. After that, they'll know who won this ongoing little fight they have."

The pastor conducting the service had apparently decided he'd had enough. Ignoring the screeching of Tabitha and Peter, he stepped up to the pulpit and began leading a closing prayer as though there wasn't a giant disturbance going on a few yards away from him. That was fine by me. I'd had enough of this funeral, and I wanted to get out of here so I could discuss Belinda more with Molly and Scott.

I had a feeling that Belinda knew something. I also had a feeling that Peter's accidental misplacement of his father's speech hadn't been so accidental. Peter clearly didn't want that speech read, but why? It had to be more than just his not wanting to subject everyone to an old man's ranting. If there was ever a time to subject people to an old man's ranting, that old man's hundredth birthday party or his funeral seemed like the appropriate time. Who could complain about putting up with the speech from a birthday party's guest of honor, or a funeral's honoree?

There must be something in that speech that Peter didn't want everyone to know, but what? Had the speech somehow referenced that Edgar cared about Tabitha, or even that Edgar planned to leave money to Tabitha?

Perhaps. Or perhaps it was something else entirely. After all, regardless of what the speech said, Edgar's will was the legal document that would determine who got his fortune. And that will would be read tomorrow for everyone to hear. Was Peter about to lose everything? Was that why he couldn't stand the very sight of Tabitha?

I could hardly wait to find out.

Chapter Seven

The next afternoon, the businesses in downtown Sunshine Springs all closed early. No one wanted to miss the will reading, myself included. As I made my way hurriedly down Main Street toward Town Hall, I passed a few bewildered tourists. They had no idea why most of downtown suddenly looked like a ghost town, but I wasn't about to stop and explain it to them. I didn't want to miss a moment of what promised to be one of the most dramatic moments Sunshine Springs had seen in quite some time.

When I got to Town Hall, the place was already packed. Tabitha and Peter were sitting in the front row of chairs with Mitch sitting between them. Mitch's presence didn't stop them from glaring at each other, and I had a feeling that no matter who got Edgar's fortune, these two would be at each other's throats the moment it was announced.

A few rows behind Mitch, I could see Grams' lime green hair. She was sitting in the midst of several of her closest friends, and they were all dressed in their Sunday best. This was quite an event for them, and I'm sure they'd been eagerly awaiting the reading of this will all day long.

Luckily for me, Molly had saved me a seat in the crowded room. She waved me over, and I slipped in next to her, Scott and Theo.

"Did I miss anything?" I asked.

"No," Molly whispered. "Edgar's lawyer hasn't started reading the will yet, and Mitch warned Tabitha and Peter that if they don't keep their hands to themselves he's going to escort them out of the room and they'll miss the reading altogether."

I couldn't help but chuckle. "Well, I'm sure that silence won't last long once they know which one of them is the lucky winner." I glanced around the room. "This is crazy. Are there any Sunshine Springs locals who aren't here?"

Molly looked around for a moment and then lowered her voice. "Belinda isn't here."

I looked around and saw that she was right. My eyes scanned over every row of chairs, and across the many faces of the people who were standing against the walls. But none of those faces was Belinda's. I saw Frank, her husband. He stood off toward one of the back corners with his arms crossed, looking very unhappy. But Belinda was nowhere to be seen.

"Strange," I said.

Edgar's lawyer was now banging his hand loudly on the podium in front of him, asking everyone to settle down. It took a few minutes, but gradually the conversations in the room quieted, and everyone gave their full attention to the lawyer.

"Thank you everyone for coming. As I'm sure you all know, Edgar asked that his will be read in public. This may seem like a strange request, but once you hear the contents of the will, I'm sure you'll understand."

The room had now become so silent that I could hear my own breathing. The lawyer's comment intrigued me. Had Edgar left some sort of message to the whole town?

Before the lawyer said anything else, however, the back door of the room opened. In the absolute silence, the door sounded abnormally loud, and everyone turned to look.

But before anyone saw who the newcomer actually was, the sound of screaming came from the front of the room. Tabitha was yelling at Peter, and Peter was starting to yell back. Mitch was yelling at both of them. I didn't know who had set off whom, but the start of the brawl at the front of the room drew everyone's attention away from the back door.

Everyone's attention but mine. I had a suspicion that I knew who the newcomer was, and I wanted to see if I was right.

I was.

In the midst of the chaos that was once again enveloping the room, Belinda had slipped in with almost no one noticing her. I glanced over at Frank, but even he hadn't seemed to realize that his wife had just joined the crowd. But Molly had noticed.

36

"It's her," Molly said. I could barely hear her over the noise of the crowd. "She did come, after all. And look what she's wearing."

"I noticed," I replied. Belinda wore a pair of dark wash jeans and a white silk blouse. She didn't have a blazer on today, which meant that her orange scarf was clearly visible. It must have been a favorite if she was wearing it two days in a row. Did she wear it all the time? Had she broken into Edgar's house and been wearing it then as well?

My suspicions were mounting, and it might have been time to finally go talk to Mitch about Belinda. But I had given up any pretense of not getting involved in this case myself. I was being sucked in by the thrill of the chase again, and I didn't want to give up my sleuthing ways. Mitch could just get over it.

Besides, I didn't have much to tell Mitch yet, even if I'd wanted to talk to him. I was suspicious of Belinda, but I still didn't know what her motive might have been to be involved in Edgar's death. And although the orange scarf did point to the fact that she may have been the burglar at Edgar's house, it wasn't conclusive proof. The flash of orange I'd seen that day might just as well have come from Peter's hat. In fact, it was more likely that it had. Peter had much more of a motivation to break into his father's house than Belinda. What could Belinda possibly have wanted to steal from Edgar?

The commotion at the front was finally settling down. Mitch was making loud threats to kick Tabitha and Peter out of the room, and those threats seemed to be working. The two of them finally quieted down and sat in their seats once again, although they didn't stop glaring at each other.

The lawyer cleared his throat and straightened his tie as he stepped up to the podium once more. He looked quite annoyed, and I had a feeling that he was starting to think that whatever he'd been paid to do this job wasn't enough. Nevertheless, he stood tall and continued on.

"As I was saying, Edgar asked that his will be read to the whole town. I will go ahead and read it now, and hopefully we can get through it without any more interruptions."

The lawyer glared down at Tabitha and Peter, but they were too busy glaring at each other to notice.

The lawyer cleared his throat once more, and then began reading. "I, Edgar Bates, being of sound mind and body, do hereby

37

make this, my last will and testament. I desire that all of my assets be liquidated. I wish for my house to be sold, and anything valuable in it to be sold as well. All proceeds from the sale, as well as the balance in all of my bank accounts, shall be combined. The total balance shall be divided as follows."

Everyone in the room leaned forward, completely silent once again. I couldn't help but glance back to see whether Belinda was still there. She was, and she looked quite worried.

The lawyer nervously cleared his throat, and then continued. "Twenty five percent of my fortune shall be bequeathed to the Sunshine Springs Police Department, to assist them in all the hard work they do to keep the citizens of Sunshine Springs safe."

A collective gasp sounded across the crowd. I wasn't sure exactly how wealthy Edgar had been, but I knew he had been wealthy enough that twenty-five percent of his fortune would amount to quite a significant sum of money. I glanced up at Mitch. He sat perfectly still, and I wished I could see his face. He must be stunned. Tabitha and Peter sat just as still. I was sure they were stunned too, but not in a good way. Their hopes for a giant payday had just been reduced by at least twenty-five percent, and that was if either of them was lucky enough to be given the remaining seventy-five percent of Edgar's fortune in total.

The lawyer continued, reading rapidly now as though worried that he might not be able to finish before complete chaos broke out. "Twenty-five percent of the proceeds from my estate shall be given to the Sunshine Springs Fire Department, to assist them in keeping the citizens of Sunshine Springs safe from the dangers of fire during the hot, dry summers that our town must endure."

Another murmur went across the crowd, but the lawyer ignored it and pressed forward.

"Twenty-five percent of the proceeds from my estate shall be given to the Sunshine Springs Independent School District, to assist them in educating our children, who, as we know, are also our future. And twenty-five percent shall be given to the Sunshine Springs Library District, so that all in Sunshine Springs can fully enjoy the benefits of reading great literature. I thank you all for the kindness you have shown me over the long life I was lucky enough to live. I hope that my gifts to the town will in some small way show the great appreciation I have toward the fine citizens of Sunshine Springs. I wish you all long, happy and healthy lives, and know that I send you all my love from the other side. Edgar Howard Bates."

For the space of several heartbeats, no one in town hall said a thing. Everyone stared in shock up at the lawyer, who began to close the folder of papers he was holding.

And then, the chaos came.

Tabitha and Peter jumped to their feet and began yelling at the lawyer that this couldn't possibly be the correct will. Mitch stood slowly, and I watched as he turned and ran his fingers through his hair in that way he did when he wasn't quite sure how to react to something. He looked out across the crowd, cracked his knuckles, and then started walking toward the door. Apparently, he was too shocked to spend time worrying about Tabitha and Peter at the moment.

I turned and glanced back at the spot where Belinda had been standing. I looked just in time to see her turning to flee out the back door.

Toward the front of the room, Grams had stood, and was fist pumping the air. Her lime green hair bounced against her head as she cheered. I couldn't tell exactly what she was saying over the rest of the noise in the room, but I could tell that she was overjoyed. And why wouldn't she be? Sunshine Springs had been her home her entire life. I'm sure she was happy to see Edgar's fortune going to help the town instead of lining the pockets of Tabitha or Peter.

Beside me, Molly was staring straight ahead. Her jaw had dropped open, but she wasn't making a sound. I grinned, and reached over to close her mouth.

"Looks like you're going to have some work to do, figuring out how to spend the windfall the library just got," I said.

Molly shook her head slowly and looked at me in wonder. "I can't believe it. I've been a librarian for ten years, and head librarian for five of those years. I can't remember a time that the library hasn't struggled to find funding. This will be such a godsend."

To my right, Scott and Theo were both laughing.

"I bet whoever killed Edgar is feeling pretty dumb right now," Theo said.

"Yup," Scott agreed. "Doesn't matter whether it was Tabitha or Peter. They're both out of luck, it seems."

At the front of the room, Tabitha and Peter were both standing by the podium and yelling at the lawyer, who looked quite haggard. He was shaking his head and pointing at the folder of papers he held, but Tabitha and Peter obviously weren't listening to him.

It served them right to lose out on Edgar's fortune. Neither one of them had truly cared for him as far as I could tell. There had been plenty of people in town who had probably loved Edgar more than Tabitha or Peter, and Edgar must have known that. He'd given his fortune to the people who would truly appreciate it.

The mystery of his murder was still unsolved. But I figured that if there was indeed an afterlife, Edgar was at peace and smiling down on the town he loved.

Chapter Eight

As soon as I closed the Drunken Pie Café the next day, I made my way to Sophia's Snips Hair Salon and Spa. Sophia Reed ran the place, and it was the only hair salon in town. It would have been pointless for anyone else to try to open one—Sophia had her market cornered. Everyone loved her beauty parlor, and it had been the number one spot for Sunshine Springs women to come and get haircuts for the last several decades.

As soon as I'd heard that Edgar's will would be read to the entire town, I had reserved an appointment at the salon for the day after. I wanted to be at the salon the next day, because I knew that would be the best place to hear all the gossip.

And it was a good thing I'd made that appointment. When I pulled into the parking lot, there wasn't a single parking spot available. I had to park on the street, and I knew the inside would be just as full.

I had let Sprinkles tag along with me, and he barked happily as we entered the hair salon. He had gotten way too used to this place. Grams often watched Sprinkles while I worked at the café so that he didn't have to hide out in the back room all day. Inevitably, whenever Grams watched him, she would bring him to the salon with her and get his nails painted. I had tried to resist at first, but now I simply shrugged my shoulders and let her. If getting my boy Dalmatian's nails painted really made Grams that happy, then it wasn't worth fighting over.

Sprinkles walked through the salon like he owned the place. As he made his rounds, he got backrubs and ear rubs from the crowd of women inside. Grams was in the salon, too. She must have had the foresight to make an appointment early as well, because she was sitting under one of the hair dryers and holding a magazine in her hand. I waved at her, and she waved back in excitement.

"Izzy, darling! So good to see you. How was your day at the café?"

I knew that by that question she really meant "What gossip did you hear today at the café?"

I shrugged. "It was a good day. Let me get checked in and I'll tell you more."

Sophia herself was standing by the front reception desk, and she waved me over.

"Come on, dear. I'll take care of you myself today. We've been quite busy, as I'm sure you've guessed."

She winked at me, and I grinned. I was excited that Sophia would be the one doing my hair today, because she would definitely have the best gossip out of all the employees. As she started shampooing my hair, I dove right in to ask her what she thought of the will reading.

I didn't even bother to act like I wasn't interested in the gossip she might have to share. She knew why I was really there. She knew why *everyone* was really there today.

"Everyone is quite excited, as you might imagine," Sophia said. "No one expected Edgar to be so generous with the city. He had become something of a grumpy old man toward the end of his life, and if I'd had to guess, I would have thought he'd leave his fortune to Tabitha just to spite his son."

"I didn't know Edgar that well," I said. "But he didn't seem that grumpy. He just seemed like the kind of guy who said what was on his mind."

Sophia laughed at that. "I suppose you're right. After one hundred years, he'd earned that right. I guess he'd also earned the right to date a thirty-year-old and then leave her with no inheritance. She must be quite disappointed."

"I'll say." I was tempted to launch right in to telling Sophia about my little visit to Tabitha. I knew Sophia would eat that story up. But I wanted to get Sophia's take on Tabitha before coloring her opinion with my own observations.

"Do you think she did it?" I asked. "Was Tabitha really the one to murder Edgar?"

"Oh, for sure," Sophia said without hesitation. "She was probably worried that if Edgar took too long to die, he'd get over his little obsession with her. Then dating him would have been a waste, because his entire fortune would be left to Peter. It makes sense, you know? Peter isn't always the nicest guy, but I can't imagine him killing his own father."

"I suppose not," I said reluctantly. "But Tabitha just seems like too much of a dumb blonde to have been able to pull off a shooting without anyone catching her. Do you think she could even figure out how to use a gun?"

Sophia paused to consider this. "I see your point, but I think Tabitha is putting on a show to make us all think she's too dumb to kill someone. You mark my words: when Mitch finally unravels this case, Tabitha will be the one at fault."

I still wasn't so sure, but I didn't see the point in pursuing that line of questioning any further. Sophia had made up her mind, and when Sophia made her mind up about something, it wasn't easy to change it.

I decided instead to ask her what she knew about Belinda. Once Sophia had finished washing my hair, and had directed me to a chair not far from where Grams was sitting at the hair dryers, I asked whether there was any gossip on Belinda.

"Belinda Simmons?" Sophia asked, looking surprised by the question. "There's not much to say about her. She's a nice enough lady, but she's lived a pretty boring life if you ask me. You know she's married to Frank, the handyman, right?"

I nodded. "Mitch told me they'd been married for a while, but that they'd been fighting a lot recently."

Sophia waved her hand dismissively. "It happens. A couple that has been together as long as Frank and Belinda will inevitably go through some rough patches. I'm sure that they'll work things out and be lovebirds again within a month or two."

I was disappointed by this answer. I'd been hoping that Sophia would have something juicy to tell me about Belinda—something that would explain why she'd been sulking around looking so suspicious lately.

But if there was anything suspicious to know about Belinda, Sophia hadn't heard about it yet. Neither had Scott. And if both of them thought there was no gossip on Belinda, then they were probably right. Nobody in town was more up-to-date on gossip than Sophia or Scott. Still, I decided to press Sophia a bit more to talk about Belinda, just in case.

"She works at the Morning Brew Café, right?"

Sophia looked up from snipping my hair and met my eyes in the mirror. "That's right. She's worked there as long as I can remember. I don't think she really needs the money anymore. Frank makes a decent enough income these days. But I suppose Belinda likes the chance to work a little and interact with the community. She's a nice enough lady, as far as I'm concerned." Sophia paused and frowned. "Although, she *has* been cheating on me lately."

"Cheating on you?" I asked.

Sophia nodded as she continued snipping at my hair. "She used to come in to the salon all the time. I've been cutting her hair for as long as I can remember. But lately, she's been going somewhere else. I don't even know where. Obviously, she has to leave Sunshine Springs to get her hair cut somewhere other than here. It's not like she's going to go to the barbershop."

I nodded. The only place to get your hair cut in Sunshine Springs other than Sophia's Snips was a barbershop on Main Street. Most of the men went to the barbershop, but none of the ladies in Sunshine Springs would be caught dead there. They all came to Sophia. If Belinda wasn't coming here, she was going to another city entirely.

It wasn't much to go on, but it was indeed a bit strange. Why would Belinda suddenly get her hair cut out of town? Where was she going, and why was she going there?

"Anyway," Sophia said. "My theory is that Belinda knows that people are gossiping about her and Frank right now. She doesn't want to deal with that gossip, so she's avoiding my salon. I'm sure once things with her and Frank settle down, she'll be back here again. She's just not comfortable in the midst of all the gossip right now, you know?"

A few feet away, I heard Grams laugh. "Ain't that the truth? Everyone loves the gossip mill until they're the one getting chewed up by it."

I nodded, but I had a feeling that there was more to Belinda's absence from the salon than just avoiding the gossip mill. Still, I didn't protest as Sophia changed subjects and started talking about something other than Belinda. It was obvious that Sophia wasn't interested in that line of conversation.

But I was interested. I had the feeling that if I figured out what was going on with Belinda, I would figure out who had murdered Edgar. Not that I thought Belinda had done it. That still seemed like a stretch to me, because I still hadn't heard anything that would make me think she had any motive to kill him. But I did think that she knew something.

There was a reason she was sneaking around, and I was going to find out what that reason was.

Chapter Nine

The next day, I took a midmorning trip over to the Morning Brew Café. It wasn't easy to get away from my own café, but when I told Molly why I wanted to go talk to Alice, the owner of the Morning Brew Café, Molly practically pushed me out the door. She was just as eager as I was to figure out what Belinda might be hiding. We both thought that maybe Alice knew something, since Belinda worked for Alice.

It was about ten-thirty in the morning when I arrived at the Morning Brew Café. The place was busy, but not overly crowded. Alice did good business, but her biggest rush came early in the morning, when people wanted to get coffee to start the day. She'd get another rush around noon, when folks stopped in for her famous sandwiches. By three p.m., she would be closed for the day. But I didn't want to wait until three p.m. to talk to her. That was one of my busiest times at the Drunken Pie Café, and I was worried that if I couldn't get away right at three when Alice closed, I wouldn't be able to catch her today. I was far too impatient to take a chance that I'd have to wait until tomorrow to talk to Alice.

When I entered the Morning Brew Café, Alice looked up in surprise.

"Izzy," she said with a quizzical look on her face. "Is the pie shop closed today?"

I shook my head no. "Molly's watching the Drunken Pie for me for a bit. I had something I really wanted to talk to you about. Do you have a minute?"

"Sure. What's up?"

I looked around the café nervously. Most of the guests who were currently sitting around drinking coffee were tourists. But there were a few locals, and I didn't want to take the chance that any of the locals would question why I had come in here to ask about Belinda.

"Could we talk in private?" I asked.

A confused look crossed Alice's face, but she didn't question me. "Sure. Jenny, can you watch the front counter for a few minutes?"

Jenny was one of the high school students who worked summer shifts at the café. Jenny nodded at Alice, and then Alice led me to the back room of the café. I was relieved that it was Jenny working today and not Belinda, because I would have been nervous to ask Alice about Belinda if the woman herself had been there. I definitely didn't want to take a chance on Belinda overhearing me talking to her boss.

Alice led me to her small office and gestured for me to sit down. She had a coffeepot back there, and asked me if I wanted her to brew me a pot. I waved her away.

"I've already had almost an entire pot today," I said with a laugh. "I probably shouldn't have any more."

Alice laughed as well. "I know the feeling. I always start my day with at least a pot. It's so hard getting up so early to open the café." She sat down and raised an eyebrow at me. "So, what can I do for you?"

I decided to jump right in. I didn't have a lot of time, and I didn't want to waste the time I did have on small talk. "I was wondering what you could tell me about Belinda?"

A shadow crossed over Alice's face. "Belinda Simmons?"

I nodded. "I heard she was your employee, so I thought you might know her pretty well."

Alice leaned back in her chair and shrugged. "Well, I thought I knew her pretty well. She worked here for over a decade. But lately she's been acting strange."

"How so?"

Alice shrugged again. "She's been acting quite sullen. She used to be this ray of sunshine. In fact, I think a lot of people came here to the café just to see her. She had the best customer service attitude you could hope for. But over the last few months she had grown grumpier and grumpier. She would hardly look at people when she took their orders, and if anyone needed help with a special order, she just about bit their head off. It was like she couldn't be bothered, which was so strange after seeing her go above and beyond for our customers for so many years. Not only that, but she started missing work shifts without warning. She used to be my most dependable employee, but over the last several weeks she missed several shifts and didn't even bother to call in. I actually just let her go last week."

"You fired her?" I asked, shocked.

Alice nodded. "That was a hard decision. She's been with me for so long that it felt like losing a family member. And besides, I don't have to tell you how difficult it is to find help in the middle of tourist season. But I had no choice. She wasn't showing up for work, and I couldn't keep expecting her to be here and then having no one to help me."

"Interesting," I said. I definitely knew what it was like to need help during tourist season. I myself had been trying to hire someone with no luck. If it hadn't been for Molly so generously helping me out, I don't know what I would have done.

Alice suddenly gave me a bit of a suspicious look. "Wait a minute. Why are you asking me so many questions about Belinda? You're not trying to steal her away as an employee for yourself, are you? I didn't fire her just so that someone else could snatch her up."

I didn't see why it mattered if someone else hired Belinda when Alice had already fired her. Alice couldn't prevent Belinda from getting another job just because she wasn't working at the Morning Brew Café. But I didn't bother pointing that out. I hadn't come here to steal away Alice's employees, whether they were currently employed by her or not. I had come to see what inside information Alice could give me about Belinda. I needed to stay in Alice's good graces, so I would say whatever I needed to say to make Alice happy.

I shook my head emphatically. "No, I'm not trying to hire Belinda—although if you do know anyone who would like to work at a boozy pie café, please send them my way. I'm desperate at this point. If it wasn't for Molly, I don't know what I'd do."

"Then why the sudden interest in Belinda?" Alice asked.

"I've seen her around a bit lately, and she always looks distraught. I'm worried about her, and I thought maybe you knew if there was something she needed help with, or something I could do for her."

It wasn't exactly the truth. I *had* seen Belinda looking unhappy, but my motive for coming here hadn't been to help her. It had been to help myself with Edgar's murder investigation.

But Alice seemed happy with my explanation. "I see. Well, I wish there was more I could tell you, but that's about all I know. Trust me, if there was something I could do to help her, then I would. She's been my employee for so long that she feels like family. But I can't help her if she won't talk to me, and she's definitely not interested in talking to me right now."

"What about Frank?" I asked. "I'm sure you've heard the gossip around town that she's having trouble in her marriage."

Alice shrugged. "Sure, I've heard that. But I don't think that's the reason she's been acting so strangely lately. She's been married a long time, and she and Frank have had their share of ups and downs. They've gone through rough patches before, and it's been hard on Belinda, of course. But it's never affected her like this. If it is her marriage that's bothering her, then they must literally be on the verge of divorce. Their arguments don't usually affect Belinda so badly."

I didn't want to comment about anyone being on the verge of divorce. I wasn't exactly one to talk when it came to that sort of thing. Besides, I was ready to get going. It was becoming clear to me that I wasn't going to learn anything new from Alice. All she could tell me was that Belinda had been in a bad mood lately, which I already knew. It was interesting to learn that she'd been fired, but what did that really tell me other than the fact that I was correct in thinking that there was something strange going on with Belinda. I was at another dead-end.

"Alright," I said to Alice. "I guess that's all I needed." I stood to leave, and Alice stood as well.

"Sorry I couldn't be more help," she said. "If there was anything I could do to help Belinda I would. But she seems determined not to be helped."

I nodded somberly. "That's rough. When someone doesn't want to be helped, there's not much you can do."

"I know," Alice said. "But lately it feels like everything is out of my control."

"Everything?" I asked. That seemed like a bit of a stretch to me. Of course, I understood that Alice was sad about Belinda, and I knew all too well the pressures of trying to run a café during tourist season while short an employee. But did that really mean *everything* was out of control?

"Well, maybe not everything," Alice admitted. "But things feel a bit chaotic lately. Think about it. We just had one of our town's most prominent citizens murdered in cold blood at his own birthday party, and the killer still hasn't been caught. How can anyone relax in times like these? I feel badly for Mitch. Can you imagine being the one who has to deal with a case like that?"

"I'm sure it's tough on him," I agreed. I definitely wasn't going to tell Alice that the reason I was actually here was that I suspected Belinda was somehow involved in the murder case. Alice would probably think I was crazy for voluntarily involving myself in this mess. And she wouldn't be the only one to think that. Mitch hated it when I poked around in police matters, and I'm sure he would have preferred that I stayed out of the investigation altogether. Luckily for me, Mitch didn't seem to have realized yet that I was trying to solve Edgar's murder. But I'm sure he would figure it out soon enough, and he wasn't going to be happy with me.

Alice was shaking her head, oblivious to the worries going on in my brain. "Sometimes, this town just doesn't seem the same anymore," she said in a wistful tone. "It used to feel like home to me, but lately things here have been so stressful that I'm wondering if living here is really all that different from living in the city. Maybe I should just move my café to San Francisco. I'd get more business and make more money. Then I could retire earlier and not have to stress at all anymore."

I smiled kindly at her. "I moved here from San Francisco, and I can tell you that the stress you would feel from being in the city wouldn't be worth it. Things might be rough here in Sunshine Springs right now, but at least it's still a community. It's still a small town where everyone knows everyone, and people take care of each other. Don't get me wrong. I had some good times in San Francisco, and that city will always have a special place in my heart. But there's something special about walking down Main Street in a place like Sunshine Springs and feeling like you're always among family. Moving here was the best decision I ever made."

Alice gave me a hopeful look. "You really think so?"

"Absolutely. I love it here. I mean, look at Edgar's will. He took care of the town he loved. That's how people are here. They take care of each other."

Alice snorted with laughter. "I don't think Peter and Tabitha are so impressed with the fact that Edgar took care of this town."

I shrugged. "Well, they got what they deserved."

"You got that right." Alice said with another snort. Then her face turned more serious "You know, Izzy...you're alright. I have to confess that when you first moved here and opened your pie shop, I was worried. I thought you were going to try to steal all my business. But it's actually been nice to have another café owner around. Oh sure, there's the Main Street Café. But Bob is a bit of a grump. He's polite enough, but I'll never be close friends with him. Maybe it's because you and I are both women, but I feel like you truly understand what I go through as a business owner."

I smiled at her. "I'm glad you feel that way. I didn't move here to try to disrupt anyone else's business, and from what I've seen, there's plenty enough business in this town to go around. The tourist season here is crazy. I can't believe how long the lines get in my pie shop some days!"

"I know what you mean," Alice agreed. "It's nice to have so much business, but by the end of the summer I'm ready for a bit of a break. Don't worry: there will still be plenty of business in the fall and winter. There's never truly an off-season here. But it *is* nice when summer passes and things slow down just a bit."

"I'll bet," I said.

And then, an idea struck me. "Hey, what would you think about doing some cross promotion? I could do a bit of advertising for the Morning Brew Café down at my pie shop, and you could advertise a bit for me here. It's true that we're both cafés, but I think the type of food we sell is different enough that people would appreciate the chance to try both places."

Alice beamed at me. "That's a great idea. Especially since I was just about to ask Jenny if she would put together some flyers for me. She's a whiz at graphic design, and I'd be a fool not to use her talents. What would you say if I asked her to put together some flyers for us?"

"I would say that sounds like a fantastic idea. Let me know what you pay her for the graphic design work, and I'll split the cost with you."

Alice was ecstatic, and I was happy that my visit to her café had been useful for her. I had felt a bit badly about taking up her time with questions about Belinda, especially when I wasn't exactly being truthful about the reason why I had those questions. But Alice seemed truly excited about the cross promotion idea. And why wouldn't she be? It would be a win-win for both of us.

I could hardly believe that not so long ago I'd been worried that I would never be accepted as a local in Sunshine Springs. Things had been rough at the beginning, but once I got past the initial barrier of being viewed as an outsider, I had quickly become family to these people. Sunshine Springs really was a great town. Edgar had known that, and that was why he'd left his fortune to the town. He might have been a grumpy old man, but he did care about this place. And that made me care about him. I was determined more than ever to find out who had killed him.

Unfortunately, chasing down information on Belinda hadn't brought me any answers. But I wasn't giving up on the case. There were plenty of other people who might have useful clues.

As I left the Morning Brew Café, I pulled out my phone and texted Scott to ask him if he could get me Peter's number.

I thought it was high time for me to have a little conversation with Edgar Bates' only son.

Chapter Ten

Tracking down Peter's phone number was easy enough. But tracking down Peter himself proved to be more of a challenge. Over the next several days, I attempted to call and text Peter multiple times, but he never answered. I even got his email address and tried to contact him that way, but I didn't receive any replies. After a few days of attempted contact with no answer, there was no denying the truth: Peter Bates was avoiding me.

And I wasn't going to let him.

I decided to pay a visit directly to his place of business. Peter owned an advertising firm with its main office located not far from the Drunken Pie Café. On a day when Molly didn't have to go work at the library in the afternoon, I begged her to close down the pie shop for me. I planned to head to Peter's advertising firm and corner him there. Molly reluctantly agreed. She wanted to come with me, but I didn't want to close down the café completely. Besides, I thought that the fewer people who showed up at the advertising firm, the easier it would be to convince Peter to talk. I already had a feeling that he was going to try to run when I arrived, and I hoped that the element of surprise would give me an advantage.

I took Sprinkles with me, and made the short drive to Peter Bates Advertising Associates. When I parked in front of the simple brick building, Sprinkles growled.

I laughed. "You're always so suspicious of everyone, boy. I don't think Peter is going to hurt me here in the middle of the business day with all of his employees around to witness things."

Sprinkles stopped growling, but he still looked unhappy as we approached the building. He looked even unhappier when I told him he had to wait outside.

"Sorry, but you know I can't take you inside. Not everyone loves dogs as much as Sophia at the hair salon. Sit over there in the shade and relax. I don't think I'll be very long, anyway. I have a feeling I'll be lucky to get even two minutes of Peter's time."

Sprinkles went to sit in the shade in a huff, and I went inside. But once inside, I was surprised to find the place almost deserted. The office had an open design, with several cubicles lined up in a large room behind the reception desk. There was one office with a closed door that I assumed belonged to Peter, but that office looked dark. Its door had frosted glass windows on it, and there didn't seem to be any lights on behind that frosted glass. The cubicles were all empty as well. The only employee I could see was the receptionist, who sat at the front desk filing her nails. She looked up in surprise when I walked in.

"Can I help you?" she asked.

"I hope so. I was actually looking for Peter. He wouldn't happen to be around, would he?"

She looked around nervously before answering. "No, he's gone for the day. In fact, everyone's gone. Peter gave them all the day off. He does that sometimes on Fridays. I have to stay to man the phone, but everyone else gets to start the weekend early."

I frowned. From what I'd heard, Peter was a bit of a slave driver when it came to his business. He didn't seem like the type to give his employees a Friday off. It wasn't possible that he'd somehow known I was coming today, was it? The idea seemed ridiculous, and yet, something about the way the receptionist was acting nervous bothered me.

I narrowed my eyes at her. "Do you have any idea where Peter might be today? I need to see him. It's a bit urgent."

The receptionist looked around nervously once again. "I'm sorry. I'm not sure where he went. He typically doesn't tell me where he's going when it's not work-related."

She looked guilty. I had a feeling she knew something, but I also had a feeling that she wasn't going to tell me. In any case, Peter wasn't there at the moment, and I was wasting my time. I thanked her and turned to leave.

Just as I turned, Sprinkles started barking like crazy. I took off at a run out the front door. I knew my pup well enough to know that a bark that sounded like that meant something. It was more than just a bored bark.

I was right. When I came out the front of the building, I saw a figure running across the parking lot. I knew immediately that it was Peter, thanks to the bright orange hat he was wearing.

"Wait!" I shouted. "I want to talk to you for a minute."

Peter didn't slow down at all. If anything, he sped up. He ran straight to a red Corvette parked under the shade of the only tree in the parking lot. He jumped in, revved up the engine, and sped away.

I kicked at the curb in defeat. Even if I had already been in my car with the engine on, there was no way I would have been able to keep up with him. A sudden surge of anger filled me. I didn't like being ignored or lied to. Peter had been ignoring me, and I was pretty sure the receptionist had lied to me. She had known Peter was here and just leaving, and I was willing to bet that she knew where he was going. I turned on my heels and started marching back into the building.

"Wait right here," I said over my shoulder to Sprinkles. "I'm going to go find out where Peter Bates is heading off to."

The receptionist had gone back to filing her nails, and clearly had not expected me to return. She jumped so violently when I stormed through the front entrance that she nearly fell out of her chair. I marched right up to the desk.

"Is...is there something else?" she stammered.

"Listen to me," I hissed at her. "I know that you must at least have some good guesses as to where Peter is heading. I need to talk to him about his father's murder investigation. So here's the deal. You can either tell me where I might find Peter, or I can grill *you* about the murder and see what you might know. It seems a bit suspicious to me that you're protecting Peter in all of this. It makes me think that you must know something about what he knows. I'd be happy to sit here and chat with you about it for a while."

The receptionist looked terrified. "I don't know anything. I swear!"

"Well, I guess you won't be too nervous about sitting down and talking to me, then."

She looked around nervously again, then looked back at me. "Are you with the police?"

I chose to not answer the question directly. No need for me to admit that I didn't actually have the authority to cross-examine her. "Like I said, I'm investigating Edgar Bates' murder. Now, would you like me to interrogate you, or would you rather tell me where Peter is so that I can interrogate him?"

"Okay, okay!" she squeaked. "He was here a few minutes ago, even though he'd given the rest of the employees the day off. But when he saw your car pull up, he took off as quickly as he could. I don't know where he was going, honest. But I do know that when he's in a bad mood, he frequently heads down to the winery's tasting room. If I had to guess, I would say that's where he's going right now."

I didn't even pause long enough to thank her for the information. I wasn't exactly in the mood to be polite at the moment. I left the office building, and ran straight toward my car.

"Come on, Sprinkles! Let's catch up with Peter Bates and figure out why he's so determined not to talk to me."

Sprinkles barked excitedly as I jumped into my car and revved up my engine. Well, revved might be a bit strong of a word. More like turned the key a few times and prayed that now would not be the moment that my ancient little coupe decided to die.

Thankfully, the engine sputtered to life, and in a few moments I was on the road. I drove as fast as I dared toward the Sunshine Springs Winery, with Sprinkles barking in excitement the whole time. When we finally made it to the winery, I was overjoyed to see Peter's red Corvette parked in front of the tasting room.

"Ha! He's here!" I yelled triumphantly. Sprinkles barked happily in response.

I decided to strategically—and very illegally—park my car so that it blocked in Peter's Corvette. I didn't want to take a chance that he would escape again.

Once my car was parked, I ran into the winery's tasting room. Sprinkles knew by now that he wasn't allowed inside this place, but he was so excited that he didn't even complain. Instead, he stood at attention right outside the door, barking excitedly as he watched me run inside.

When I got inside, Peter was already standing and turning to run. He must have heard Sprinkles and realized I was coming. In his haste to leave, he knocked over the barstool he'd been sitting on. But he didn't slow down to fix it. Instead, he ran full speed toward the door, already pulling his keys out of his pocket. Shocked tourists scrambled to get out of his way, even as I scrambled to block the exit.

But the fact that I was standing in the doorway didn't slow him down, either. He pushed past me and made a beeline for his car, ignoring my yelp of pain. Sprinkles saw him coming out and began barking even louder.

I regained my balance and turned to run after Peter. "Wait! I just want to ask you a few questions. Why are you avoiding me like this?"

"Leave me alone!" Peter roared. "I don't want to talk to you, and I don't have to. You're not the police!"

He was already opening his car door before he realized that he was blocked in. He let out a long stream of curses that would have made even the most hardened sailor blush, and then he took off running in the direction of the grapevines. I ran after him.

I wasn't in the best shape of my life, to be honest. Eating pie for breakfast pretty much every day wasn't doing anything for my mile time, and the leather flats I was wearing didn't make the best running shoes. But Peter didn't seem to be in the best shape of his life either. He wasn't exactly fat, but he definitely had a bit of a stomach pooch going on. Not only that, but his footwear wasn't much better than mine. He had on a pair of black dress shoes that were quickly turning gray from the dust he was kicking up as he ran.

I gritted my teeth together and tried to ignore the sweat that almost instantaneously started beading up on my face. The late summer sun beat down on me, and within moments I could feel myself overheating. Still, I persisted. I gritted my teeth together and chased after Peter as he disappeared down a long row of grapevines. I would outrun him, if it took every last ounce of strength I had. This might be my only chance to talk to him, since he seemed so determined to avoid me.

His determination not to talk to me made me more suspicious than ever. If he'd had nothing to do with his father's death, and he didn't know anything about who had shot Edgar, then why was he so quick to run? Was it because he was angry at being written out of the will and didn't want to have to answer questions about that? Or was it because he was hiding something deeper?

I was going to find out.

I slowly gained on him as he stumbled through the grapevines. At first, I kept calling after him to wait. But eventually, I was too out of breath to waste any precious oxygen on words. It's not like those words were helping, anyway. Peter wasn't answering me, and my yells only served to frighten him into running faster.

He did glance over his shoulder now and then to see whether I was still following him. I was, and I wasn't giving up. He had to be feeling the heat and the pain of exertion just as much as I did, if not more. I just had to outlast him.

A few moments later, I caught a lucky break. Peter turned around to look at me once again, and as he turned he caught his foot on a clump of dirt. He tripped and went tumbling straight into the ground. As he cried out in pain, I cried out in triumph. Finally, I would get my chance to talk to him.

"Now maybe you'll listen to me!" I said as I ran up to where he had fallen. But the triumphant grin faded from my face when he suddenly flipped open a pocketknife and pointed it in my direction.

"I'll never listen to you," he growled. "And don't make me prove it!"

Chapter Eleven

I skidded to a halt at the sight of the knife, and took a few steps backward.

Suddenly, chasing after a potential murderer in an empty row of grapevines didn't seem like the smartest idea I'd ever had. I hadn't believed that Peter was the most likely murderer, but the fact that he'd just pulled a knife on me had ratcheted up my suspicion level a few notches. Sure, it was only a pocketknife. But I was sure he would still be able to do quite some damage with it if he tried.

Now, the beads of sweat on my forehead weren't all from the heat of the sun or the exertion of running.

To my relief, I heard a sudden growling sound behind me. In the excitement of chasing after Peter, I had completely forgotten that I'd brought Sprinkles with me to the winery. I had never been so happy to see my Dalmatian. Sprinkles might not be the world's best guard dog, but he was big and he had sharp teeth. I felt confident that he could take on Peter and a puny little pocketknife. I stood taller, and boldly took a step forward.

"There's no need to threaten me," I said. "I just want to ask you a few questions. That shouldn't bother you so much, unless of course you have something to hide. Are you the one who shot your father?"

As I'd hoped, that question got quite a reaction from Peter.

"Of course I didn't shoot my father!" he roared at me. His face, shirt, and stupid orange hat were all drenched in sweat. His skin was a bright red color, although I wasn't sure whether the red hue was due to anger, overexertion, or a combination of both. Either way, I was starting to feel a bit less scared of him by the moment. He was worn out, and if he tried to attack me, it would be a piece of cake for Sprinkles to take him out. I think Peter knew that, because he slipped the pocketknife back into his pocket.

"If you're so innocent in all of this," I asked. "Then why don't you want to talk to anyone?"

"Why do you think?" he asked in a sarcastic tone. "How would you feel if your father had just been murdered, you lost out on your inheritance, and some crazy blonde bimbo was blaming you for ruining her life just because her attempts at being a gold digger didn't yield any actual gold? Would you feel like talking in that situation?"

"Fair enough," I said. "But all you're doing by hiding is making yourself look more suspicious."

"More suspicious to whom? You? You'll have to forgive me if I don't really care. I've already given a statement to the police. What more do you want me to do?"

I took a deep breath and decided to attempt to win Peter over with kindness. Spice wasn't working, but maybe sugar would. I raised my hands in a gesture of surrender, and tried to make my voice sound soothing.

"Look, I understand how you feel. I myself was once falsely accused of murder. I know it isn't fun, which is why I want to help you. I'm not with the police, and Mitch doesn't know I'm here. I'm just trying to get to the truth of things, and figure out who actually shot your dad. Don't you want to know?"

Peter still eyed me suspiciously. "I already know. Tabitha did it, and the worst part is that she killed him for nothing. She wanted his money, but my dad was smart enough not to leave her anything. Of course, I got nothing either. That was probably all thanks to Tabitha. My dad was so tired of us arguing with each other that he wrote us both out of his will. I just wish he'd lived long enough to realize what a con artist she was."

"I agree with you that Tabitha is the most likely perpetrator. But Mitch doesn't have any hard proof, and until he does it's going to be difficult to convict her. I'm trying to find proof."

Peter sneered at me. "And you think talking to me is going to help you find it? Don't you think Mitch has already gotten all the information he can from me? I told him all I know and he still hasn't found anything to nail Tabitha with. Why would you do any better?"

"Because I think differently from Mitch. He's always in police mode. I think outside his little law enforcement box. Maybe I'll see something he didn't."

Peter pulled off his ridiculous orange hat, ran his fingers through his sweaty hair, and replaced the hat. I was wishing I had a hat myself at the moment. The sun was beating down so strongly, and there was nowhere out here to hide from it. But I wasn't leaving until I got Peter to talk. I wasn't about to pass up this opportunity.

Peter stood slowly and brushed the dirt off his pants as best he could. "If I answer your stupid questions, will you leave me alone?"

I raised my right hand. "Scout's honor."

"Fine. Then ask. But be quick about it. I have better things to do than stand out here melting in the middle of the vineyard."

"I understand. In fact, let's start walking back while we talk. I'm melting as well."

Peter grunted and started walking back toward the tasting room at a brisk pace. I knew I had to talk quickly before he changed his mind.

"I was just wondering whether you could tell me if your father had any enemies? Was there anyone other than Tabitha who might have wanted to kill him?"

Peter looked over at me and glared. "I thought you said you were trying to prove that Tabitha killed him. Sounds to me like you're trying to find someone else who might be responsible."

"I'm just trying to cover all my bases," I said hurriedly. "If we show that Tabitha was the only one with motive, then it strengthens the case against her."

This seemed to satisfy Peter. "I don't think he had any enemies. I'm sure if you've been asking around, then you know that there were people who thought he was a grumpy old man. But I don't think he really had any enemies. Actually, I don't think he had any enemies *or* friends at the end."

I looked over at Peter in surprise. "You don't think he had any friends? Didn't you see how the whole town came out for his hundredth birthday celebration?"

"Of course the whole town came. It was a big social event. People were coming to hang out with their other friends in the town, not necessarily for my dad."

I frowned. "It seemed to me like people were genuinely excited to celebrate him."

"Maybe it seemed that way because people were excited for the party. But my dad didn't have many people he was truly close to

61

anymore. That was all Tabitha's doing. She had really changed my dad. She was trying to cut him off from everyone who cared about him so that she could get his fortune for herself. Any time he tried to hang out with friends she flipped out at him and told him that he didn't love her. She probably would have loved it if she could have found a way to cancel his hundredth birthday party altogether. But the wheels for that had been in motion for so long that there was too much momentum for even her to stop."

Peter paused for a moment, and when he started speaking again, his voice caught in his throat. "That party was the first time in a long time I'd seen my dad happy. I only wish I hadn't been so impatient with him that night. If I'd known it would be the last time I saw him alive, I wouldn't have given him such a hard time about that stupid speech of his."

The mention of the speech bothered me. I had felt for a while that there was more to that speech than Peter was letting on, and I decided that now was as good a time as any to press him on that point.

"What was in that speech, anyway?"

"Just the ramblings of an old man. It would have been a waste of time for him to give that speech, yes. But it would have made him happy."

"Don't you think it would have made him happy to know it was read at his funeral?" I insisted.

I wasn't letting Peter off the hook so easily. If he really thought the speech meant a lot to his dad, why had he not made sure that it was read at his dad's funeral?

Peter gave me a withering look. "I don't think it matters much what happened at his funeral. The man is dead. Funerals are for the living. And trust me, none of the living in Sunshine Springs want to hear that stupid, rambling speech."

I was silent for a moment. I didn't know what to make of Peter. He sounded like a truly heartbroken son one minute, and then the next minute sounded like he couldn't have cared less about his father. Out of the corner of my eye, I saw him pull off his hat and run his fingers through his hair before replacing it once again. The orange of the hat made me think of the break-in I'd witnessed the day I visited Tabitha, and I decided to ask him about that in a roundabout way.

"Have you been back to your father's house at all since he died?"

I watched carefully to see how Peter would react. His eyes darkened with anger, but the question didn't seem to rattle him any more than any other question I'd asked him.

"No, I haven't been. I've tried. I wanted to go and see about getting some things that are important to me. You know, old family photos and things like that. But Tabitha won't let me in. She claims I'm trying to take valuables that I have no right to. She has no right to them, either. You heard the will: everything of value is supposed to be sold so that the proceeds can benefit the town. But Tabitha isn't going to leave until the sheriff forcefully evicts her. It makes me so angry that I can't get in. I'm not even trying to take anything of value. I just want my family photographs. Is that too much to ask?"

"No, of course not," I said soothingly. I wasn't convinced that Peter wouldn't take anything of value from the house if given the chance, but it was pointless to tell him that. I would only make him angry. So instead, I asked, "Have you talked to Mitch about getting into the house? Maybe he can help you. If he escorts you in to get your photographs, Tabitha won't be able to protest. And I'm sure Mitch wouldn't have any objections to helping you get items of sentimental value."

Peter scowled at me. "I don't even want to talk to Mitch. He's being extraordinarily unhelpful. Tabitha told him that there was a break-in at the house, and Mitch is convinced that I'm the one who broke in. He's on my case to stay away from the house, and I don't think he would help me get anything from inside. The whole thing is absolutely ridiculous. Trust me, if I really wanted to get in, I wouldn't sneak around behind Tabitha's back. I'd just march up to the front door and push my way past her. What is she going to do? Call Mitch and complain? She doesn't have a right to be there any more than I do."

I tried to see from the expression on Peter's face whether he was telling the truth or not, but all I could see on his face was anger. And he did have a point. If he went to his house and forced his way in, what was Tabitha going to do? Call the police and ask them to remove Peter? Even before the will had been read, she didn't exactly have strong standing to ask for him to be kicked out of the house. She had never actually owned that place.

But if Peter hadn't broken in, then who had? And what were they looking for? I decided to ask him that very question, but when I did he merely shrugged.

"Beats me," he said. "There's a lot of valuable stuff in my dad's house. Someone probably thought they could make off with something and sell it to make a quick buck."

He was right. The break-in might have been a simple burglary. If Peter had indeed been the one breaking in, he certainly didn't have a reason to admit that to me.

We were almost back to the tasting room by then, and I didn't feel that the conversation had helped me that much. Nothing Peter had said had swayed my opinion of him one way or the other. I decided to use my remaining time to ask him about Belinda.

"Do you know if your father was friends with Belinda Simmons?"

Peter looked surprised by the sudden change of subject. He shook his head slowly. "I don't think so. Her husband Frank had recently done quite a bit of remodeling work on my dad's kitchen. I only know that because I know Tabitha complained to my dad about it. She thought it was a waste of money. Of course, what she really meant was that she didn't want him spending any more money on the house so that there would be more money for her when he died. But anyway, I think Frank and my dad were pretty good buddies. Since Tabitha had been trying to cut people off, my dad didn't see many people. But for a while, Frank was at the house almost every day to work on the kitchen. I think my dad appreciated having him there, even just to have some company."

"But Belinda wouldn't have been there, right? Just Frank."

"Right. Belinda wouldn't have had a reason to be there. She never helped Frank with remodeling work as far as I know. She preferred to spend time working at the Morning Brew Café. She's been an employee there for years, you know?"

I knew. I also knew that Belinda had been fired from the Morning Brew Café, but I decided not to tell Peter that. He'd seemed genuinely surprised by the question about Belinda, and he hadn't had much to tell me. But the fact that Frank had been connected to Edgar meant that there might indeed be a reason that Belinda had crossed Edgar's path recently.

It wasn't much to go on, true. But I was grasping at straws right now. Since I didn't have any other good leads at the moment, maybe it was time to pursue my suspicions of Belinda. I had a hard time believing that it was a coincidence that she had been acting so strangely right around the time Edgar died. Did she have a deeper connection to him than Peter or anyone else realized? I needed to find out more.

Back at the tasting room, I moved my car so that Peter could leave. He hardly said another word to me before jumping into his car and speeding out of the parking lot. I watched him go in a cloud of dust, and my shoulders slumped in defeat. I hadn't learned much from him, and I had definitely made him angry. I felt like a failure of a detective.

But I wasn't giving up. Edgar's killer, whoever he or she might be, was still on the loose. Edgar deserved justice, and Sunshine Springs deserved safe streets. I wasn't going to rest until this case was solved, and that meant it was time to track down Belinda.

Chapter Twelve

As usual, my sleuthing attempts would have to be put on hold while I ran my pie shop. I couldn't just make Molly take care of everything day after day. Besides, as much as I was itching to find Belinda and get her to talk to me, I had to admit that I did miss my pie shop when I wasn't there. Even though everyone in town had a love-hate relationship with the tourists, I did enjoy the chance to talk to new people every day.

Not only that, but many of the locals in Sunshine Springs were starting to become regulars. By now, there were several people whose order I knew before they said a word. A few of my regulars even liked to order boozy pie at nine a.m. I didn't judge. There wasn't that much alcohol in a pie anyway since it got baked out. I still preferred nonalcoholic pies in the morning, but, hey. This was wine country. If someone wanted to live it up, there weren't many better places to do so.

The day after my confrontation with Peter, Molly had a lot of work to do at the library. I had to run the pie shop by myself, and I hardly had a moment to breathe. I would manage, but days like today really made me wish that I'd had better luck finding someone to hire as an employee. It also made me realize that Alice had to have been extraordinarily frustrated with Belinda. No one would fire an employee in the middle of tourist season unless they absolutely had to.

The day hummed along, and around two p.m. there was finally a bit of a lull in the shop. A few customers sat at the café tables eating pie, drinking wine, or sipping on coffee. But nobody was waiting to order, and no one needed anything from me at that exact moment. I took the opportunity to lean against the counter and catch my breath.

But that moment of quiet didn't last long. Just a few seconds after I'd poured myself a nice big drip coffee, the bell above the door jingled. I put a smile on my face, and reminded myself to be grateful for every customer. Better to be too busy than not busy enough.

But when I saw who had just walked into my pie shop, I nearly gasped. Frank Simmons, Belinda's husband, stood in the Drunken Pie Café, looking uncertainly around. I'd never seen him in the café before. I supposed it was possible he had come in one of the few times that Molly was running the café by herself. But she hadn't done that very often, and I was pretty sure that she would have mentioned it if she'd seen him recently. She knew all about my suspicions of Belinda.

I felt a spark of fear go through me as I watched Frank. Why had he suddenly shown up now? Was it coincidence, or had he heard that I'd been asking around town about Belinda? Was he here to confront me and tell me to leave his wife alone? Even if they were fighting, he probably wouldn't appreciate someone accusing her of being somehow involved in Edgar's murder. I gulped back my fear and tried to look calm as he started walking toward the front counter.

"Can I help you?" I asked brightly, hoping that my voice didn't betray the worry I felt.

Frank looked around again with a lost expression on his face, and I relaxed a bit. He didn't look like a man who had come here to chew anyone out. He looked more like someone lost in an unfamiliar city, even though he was a local here. He stared at the pie case for a moment before looking over at me.

"Could I talk to the shop owner, please?"

"That would be me," I said, and extended a hand out. "I'm Isabelle James. Most people call me Izzy."

He reached out to shake my hand, gripping it much harder than necessary. Something was definitely making him nervous.

"Oh, right. I should have known. I've seen you around town a lot, but I didn't realize you were the one who owned this place."

"I am indeed. What can I do for you?"

"I was wondering if you do special orders." Frank looked down at his hands as he spoke, nervously pressing his fingers against each other.

That surprised me. I don't know what I thought he'd been about to ask, but that definitely wasn't it. And why was he so nervous to ask a simple question like that?

"Yes, we do special orders from time to time. Is it for an event? I'll just need enough advance notice to make sure I have time to prepare everything properly."

"No, it's not for a big event. It's actually for my anniversary with my wife."

"Belinda?" I asked. I couldn't keep the surprise out of my voice. I'd heard so much about the troubles that Frank and Belinda were having that it seemed strange to me that he wanted to give her an anniversary surprise. But maybe Frank wanted the marriage to work, and thought that an anniversary was the perfect time to try to win his wife's heart back.

Frank looked a little bit relieved. "Oh, you know Belinda?"

I nodded. "I do. From the Morning Brew Café."

As soon as the words were out of my mouth, I regretted bringing up the place. It probably wasn't the smartest of ideas to bring up the café Belinda had just been fired from, but Frank didn't seem bothered. Instead, his eyes brightened.

"Of course. I forget how many people she meets through working there. I keep telling her that we don't need the money, but she keeps working there, anyway. She says it's not about the money. She claims she truly loves the job."

I frowned slightly. Frank apparently didn't know that Belinda had been fired, and I certainly wasn't going to be the one to tell him. But now I was even more suspicious of Belinda. Why was she sneaking around so much, and why was she hiding things from her husband? Being fired from your longtime job was a pretty big deal.

"Yes, the café certainly seems like a lovely place to work," I said, and then quickly changed the subject. "So, what kind of pie do you want to order for your anniversary? We have quite a large menu to choose from. If you see any that you like up on the board, let me know. I can make sure to have one freshly made for you on the day of your anniversary."

"That would be great," Frank said. "Could you make me a key lime margarita pie? Our anniversary is August thirtieth, so I would need it for that day. And do you have any way to write on it or decorate it? I want it to be special."

"I don't generally write on pies, but I could get some icing and do a special message if you'd like. The key lime pie has a smooth surface on top, so an icing message would work nicely."

"Great! Could you write 'Happy anniversary, Belinda. Thank you for the best twenty-five years of my life'?"

"Of course! It's your twenty-fifth anniversary? That's a big one."

Frank looked at me with sad eyes. "It is, but it might be our last. If you've been around Sunshine Springs for any amount of time, I'm sure you've heard people talking about the troubles Belinda and I are having."

I didn't want to admit to gossiping about him, but I knew it would be useless to deny it. The gossip train in Sunshine Springs was an unstoppable machine. I would have to have been deaf not to have heard something about Belinda and him, but I tried to downplay the issue.

"I've heard people say you guys were going through a rough spot," I admitted. "But everyone does, right? And maybe this anniversary will be a good chance for you to start over."

I smiled brightly at him, but he didn't smile back. Instead, he sighed and ran his fingers through his hair.

"I hope so, but I have to say I'm not so confident. I don't know what happened, honestly. We've had our rough spots, sure. But we've always pulled through them. But this seems different. She's so distant, and I don't know why. It all started around the time I began a remodeling project for Edgar Bates. I'm sure you know of him, since his murder has been the biggest news around here lately."

I could hardly keep the excitement from showing on my face. It was all I could do to keep from leaning forward and begging Frank to tell me everything he knew about Edgar. But I managed to control myself, and merely nodded. "I know about Edgar. Such a tragedy."

"Right," Frank said. "I'm sure that thirty-year-old gold digger he had was the one who killed him off. I tried to tell Edgar to get rid of her, but he wouldn't listen. He said that he'd lived a long life, and if he wanted to have a little bit of fun at the end of it then no one had the right to stop him. At least he didn't leave her his fortune. I was really worried for a while that he was going to do that."

"No, but he was quite generous with his gifts to the town," I said. "He must have been a really good man. Unfortunately I didn't get the chance to know him well since I only recently moved here."

"He was a very good man," Frank said. "I still can't believe he's gone. Of course, we all knew he'd be gone soon enough, given how old he was. But it's such a shock that he died the way he did, and it's so sad that we were robbed of the last precious days we might have had with him."

Frank looked down at his hands, and I could see him trying to compose himself. I could also see my chance at learning more about Edgar slipping away. As much as I sympathized with Frank's grief, I couldn't stand to let this opportunity go.

"But you did get to spend a lot of time with him at his home recently, didn't you?" I prompted.

Frank looked back up at me. "Yeah. I remodeled his kitchen, and I'd often stay and spend some time with him even when my work was done. He seemed lonely, and I genuinely enjoyed hanging out with him. But that was when Belinda started pulling away. At the time, I couldn't figure out what her problem was. But now that Edgar's gone, part of me wonders whether she knew something about the murder. Did she know what Tabitha was planning? I can't believe that she would have known and not said anything, but maybe I don't know her as well as I thought I did after twenty-five years. Since Edgar's death, she's only become more distant."

"Have you asked her about it?"

"Yes, I've tried to get her to talk to me. I've told her that if she knows something she should go to the police, but she swears I'm crazy and that there's no reason she would know anything about Tabitha or Edgar's murder."

Frank put his hands in the air in a gesture of helplessness, and then his cheeks turned a little red. "Anyway, I'm sorry. I've said too much, and I'm sure you don't want to be burdened with my silly problems. If you could just make that pie, I'd be so grateful."

"Of course," I said. "I'll put it on my calendar, and you can pay for it when you pick it up. I'm sure it will do wonders to help things between you and Belinda."

Frank murmured his thanks, and after a few more polite words he shuffled his way out of the pie shop.

Things were picking up once again, but it was hard for me to focus on anything other than thoughts of Belinda. After my conversation with Frank, I knew that Belinda must know something. If she wasn't the killer, then she at least had some idea of who was. I definitely needed to talk to her, but now I realized that talking to

Tabitha might help, too. Frank had mentioned that he thought Belinda might have somehow known something about Tabitha. If that was the case, did Tabitha know something about Belinda?

It was a possibility, and Tabitha might be getting out of town soon. She had no reason to stay since Edgar was dead and she wasn't getting any of his fortune. I decided to go talk to her that very afternoon after the pie shop closed. I wanted to ask her about Belinda in person, and see the look on her face when I brought up Belinda's name. If Tabitha looked concerned by the fact that I was speaking of Belinda, then maybe that would tell me that I was on the right track.

The next few hours seemed to fly by, and I was actually quite thankful that the shop was too busy for me to stand around and watch the clock. I could hardly wait to get to Tabitha. With any luck, I had finally smashed through one of the roadblocks in this murder investigation.

Maybe I would solve things before Mitch even knew I was involved. That would be fun. I giggled to myself as I imagined the look on his face if I walked into the police station with hard evidence of who had committed the crime. Hey, a girl can dream, right?

At five p.m., I closed up the pie shop faster than I ever had before. After quickly running through all of my closing duties, I grabbed a giant slice of lemon vodka pie and packaged it up. Then I whistled to Sprinkles, who had been dozing in the back room all this time.

"Come on, boy. Time for us to make a little social call to the woman who most likely murdered Edgar Bates."

Chapter Thirteen

I half expected Edgar Bates' house to be dark when I arrived. Despite Peter's insistence that Tabitha wasn't going to leave until Mitch kicked her out, I suspected that she might actually be ready to get out of Sunshine Springs as fast as she could. After all, she knew for sure now that there was no fortune coming her way.

But I'd underestimated Tabitha. When I arrived, she was definitely still there. The lights were all on in the house, and her little sports car was parked out front. I knew it was hers, because it was hot pink. I would have bet my pie shop that no one else in Sunshine Springs had a hot pink car. Grams was the only other person I knew who would drive something so garish, but right now Grams drove a boring, black sedan.

I hadn't noticed the car the last time I was here, which meant it must have been in the garage. Right now, the garage door was open and the lights inside the garage were on. I could see several moving boxes stacked in the space that should have held a car, but Tabitha herself was nowhere to be seen.

I parked my little white coupe behind Tabitha's car, and I thought that my poor old vehicle had never looked as sad and decrepit as it did next to such a shiny pink automobile. My car's appearance couldn't be helped, though, and I didn't want to waste time worrying about it.

I got out of my car, grabbed the pie box, and did my best to dust any residual flour off my work pants. Sprinkles jumped out of the car after me, his damp black nose sniffing the air curiously. He let out a low growl, and I frowned. I had learned by now that it wasn't a good idea to ignore Sprinkles' growls.

"What is it, boy?" I asked.

He growled again, and took a step closer to me. A shiver ran down my spine. I realized that I was about to go into the house of a potential murderer, and no one knew where I was. Sometimes, I got too comfortable in Sunshine Springs. It was such a charming small town that it was easy to forget that someone in this town had recently killed one of the town's oldest citizens.

"Maybe I should at least tell someone where I am," I said to Sprinkles.

I pulled my cell phone out of my pocket and sent a quick text to Molly: *Hey! I know you're busy at the library tonight, but I just wanted to let you know I'm going to try to talk to Tabitha again. I'll let you know if I find out anything interesting!*

I sent the text with a wince, knowing that Molly wouldn't be happy that I was running off to sleuth without her again. But I knew she wouldn't be able to join me tonight, and I didn't want to take a chance on waiting any longer. What if Tabitha hightailed it out of town?

At least Molly would know where I was, and if I didn't show up at the pie shop the next day then the police would know where to find my body. I shivered at the gruesome thought, and quickly made my way to ring the doorbell before I could chicken out. With any luck, Tabitha would be a dog lover and would be willing to let me bring Sprinkles inside with me. I would feel a lot better if I could keep him by my side.

But when Tabitha answered the door and saw Sprinkles, she made a face. "I can't stand dogs. They're such mangy beasts."

Sprinkles growled, but I shook my head at him. "No, Sprinkles. Don't be rude. You know not everyone is a dog lover, and growling at them isn't going to change their minds. Wait out here like a good boy, and I'll give you some pie when we get home."

Sprinkles stopped growling, but the glare he gave me told me that he wasn't on board with my decision to head inside by myself. It probably wasn't the smartest idea, but if I wanted a chance to talk to Tabitha, I didn't have much of a choice. I gulped back my fear and forced a giant smile onto my face.

"I had some leftover lemon vodka pie today, and I thought you might like some. I wanted to come check on you and see how you were holding up. The last few days must have been so difficult for you."

Tabitha's face softened. "Oh, you have no idea. It's been awful. Come on in. I'm sorry about your dog, really. It's just that I'm not an animal person. Animals give me so much anxiety."

"It's all right," I lied. "He'll be fine outside." Secretly, I was thinking about how I didn't trust anyone who didn't like dogs.

I followed Tabitha into the kitchen, where she'd led me the last time I was here. But things looked different now. I couldn't ignore how many moving boxes were stacked all over the place.

"I guess you're heading out of town?" I asked, although it was more of a statement than a question.

Tabitha glanced over the boxes, and then gave me a wary look.

"Yes, I'm leaving. There's nothing left for me here. Besides, Mitch has been on my case that I need to get out of the house since it wasn't left to me. Honestly, no one here has any sympathy for me. My whole life has been turned upside down, and they can't even give me time to properly pack and get out of here."

"Looks like you're packing quite a bit." I didn't feel a lot of sympathy for Tabitha. In fact, I wanted to ask if Mitch knew how much stuff she was taking, but I didn't go that far. I wasn't about to get into an argument over what she was entitled to take as she left. Mitch could deal with that.

Tabitha narrowed her eyes at me, and I could see the challenge in them. She was daring me to say anything more. "Well, I had quite a bit of stuff here. I spent the last several months in this house, as you know. All of my clothes, jewelry, and other belongings were here, and those things are still mine. They're not considered part of the estate. Neither are things that Edgar had given me as gifts. The lawyers can't take that away from me!" She slammed her fist on the island, and I jumped backward, startled.

As I jumped, I accidentally hit my arm on a box that had been sitting on the very edge of the island. It moved a little bit, and I rushed to move it back so that it wouldn't fall over. But I overcorrected, moved too quickly, and accidentally knocked the whole thing onto the floor.

I watched in horror as the box seemed to fall in slow motion. I cringed, waiting for the sound of shattering glass I was sure I was about to hear. The box had been in the kitchen, and had felt relatively heavy when I touched it. It must have held dishes or glassware, and I was sure that Tabitha would be furious with me for breaking things.

74

But when the box hit the floor, there was no sound of shattering glass. Instead, I watched as hundreds of photos went sliding out of the side of the box. I felt a rush of relief, but that relief only lasted a moment. As I looked at the photos, I saw that they were not the sort of thing Tabitha would have wanted me to see.

All of the pictures I was looking at appeared to be of Tabitha—and she was wearing hardly any clothing in any of them. In fact, she looked to be absolutely naked in several, although her hands were carefully covering up her most important bits. I gawked at the photos, and then gawked up at her.

Her eyes were blazing with anger. "How dare you!" she screamed at me. "Those are personal. You have no right to come over here and snoop!"

"I'm sorry," I stammered. "I wasn't trying to snoop! It was an accident. My hand caught on the box and it toppled over. I had no idea there were photographs in there. I thought the box had dishes in it."

Tabitha rushed around the island to start throwing the photographs back into the box. It was difficult for her to do, because she was wearing a tight dress and her signature sky-high heels. I wondered why in the world she insisted on wearing heels even at home where no one would see her. I also wondered whether I should try to help her pick up the photographs, or whether that would make it worse. She clearly didn't want me to see them, and if I helped her pick them up I was only going to see more of them.

Paralyzed by indecision, I stood watching helplessly as she fumbled with the mountains of pictures. The more she tried to put them away, the more the piles tumbled over and I could see just how risqué the photos were. I considered leaving, but then decided against it. If Tabitha wasn't going to kick me out, then I would stay and hope that I could somehow salvage this situation. I still wanted to ask her about Belinda, and I was pretty sure at this point that I wasn't going to get another chance. Tabitha was obviously trying to leave town quickly with as much of Edgar's stuff as possible.

So I stood there, waiting to see how long it would take Tabitha to fix the mess I had created. As she worked to throw the photographs back into the box, she got angrier and angrier. Finally, she threw her hands up in the air and then started laughing hysterically. She sounded crazy, and now I was really sure that I would be better off leaving.

And yet, I stayed.

"Are you okay?" I asked hesitantly.

Tabitha kept laughing for a few more moments, and then she looked at me, wiping tears from her eyes. I wasn't sure whether the tears were from laughter or from anger.

"Oh, forget it," she said. "It's no use trying to hide these photos from you. You've seen them all now. And you clearly see that I was a playgirl of sorts."

I wasn't sure what to say. "That's quite surprising," I finally managed, and then immediately regretted the words. That could definitely be taken as an insult.

But Tabitha didn't seem insulted. She kept laughing and wiping at her eyes. Finally, she quieted down and shrugged.

"I suppose it's surprising to you prudes from Sunshine Springs, but it's really nothing for me to be ashamed of."

I kept my mouth shut, not bothering to tell her that I hadn't lived in Sunshine Springs until this summer. I'd seen my fair share of risqué things in the city of San Francisco, and I certainly didn't judge Tabitha for what she did in her private life. But I had to admit that I was curious whether old Edgar had known about this.

As if reading my mind, Tabitha crossed her arms and gave me a challenging look.

"Edgar knew that I sometimes...modeled. He had no problem with it. In fact, he thought it was cool that he had snagged such a beautiful model." Tabitha smiled, and then frowned. "But not cool enough that he left me anything in his will."

Tabitha angrily threw more piles of photos back into the box. I saw a chance to redeem myself, and to possibly still have a chance to ask her about Belinda.

I smiled warmly. "Hey, it's no big deal. It's your business if you want to model. There's no law against that."

Tabitha looked relieved. "Of course not. There's no law against modeling." Her eyes darkened as she threw more photos back into the box. "But there is a law against breaking into homes."

I didn't bother to mention that this wasn't her home, but I was interested that she'd brought up the break-in again. "Did the police catch the burglar?"

Tabitha scowled. "Of course not. The police here are completely lazy and incompetent. And what's worse is that whoever the burglar is has been trying to break in again. The other day I came

76

home from the grocery store and someone was running out of the house. I'm sure it was Peter. I saw something orange, and he's always wearing that awful orange hat. He's probably been trying to take off with as many valuables as he can before everything goes to auction."

I thought back to what Peter had told me about trying to get his photographs. I wondered if he'd been here trying to get sentimental items, or if he'd been trying to take valuables. It's not like Tabitha could complain about that. She was clearly taking much more than she was entitled to. Even if she'd lived here for years, I didn't think that all of the stuff she was packing up belonged to her. The house was starting to look a bit bare. But again, not really my problem. I was more interested in figuring out who committed the murder than in policing how much anyone took from the house.

"Well," I said soothingly. "Soon enough you'll be all moved out and have moved on with your life. Peter won't be your problem anymore."

"Ain't that the truth," Tabitha said. She had finally finished putting the photographs back in the box, and she stood to her feet with just a bit of wobble.

"Now," she said. "What about that pie? I could use some straight-up vodka, but I don't suppose you brought any of that with you?"

I shook my head. "Sorry. Just a vodka pie."

Tabitha let out a dramatic sigh. "I guess that will have to do."

She opened the box, grabbed a fork, and started eating the slice without bothering to put it on a plate.

I probably should have made small talk and tried to butter her up a little bit before asking her more questions, but I was worried that I was running out of time. I decided to jump straight into my questions about Belinda.

"This kitchen is beautiful," I commented. "Peter told me that it was remodeled right before Edgar died."

Tabitha's eyes darkened. "Yeah. What a waste. But I guess it's not my problem anymore. The old kitchen was fine, but Edgar insisted that a new set of countertops and cabinets would do wonders for the place." She rolled her eyes. "I think he just wanted to hang out with Frank, the guy who did the remodeling. That guy was so weird."

"What about Frank's wife? Did you ever meet her?"

77

"Belinda?" Tabitha asked, narrowing her eyes at me once again. "No, I never met her."

"But you know her name," I pointed out.

For a brief moment, I saw panic flicker across Tabitha's eyes. She hid it quickly, but I saw it and felt a rush of excitement. I was definitely onto something.

Tabitha shrugged. "Of course I knew her name. Her husband was here all the time talking to Edgar. Belinda was bound to come up now and then."

"What sort of things did Frank say about her?" I asked. "Did he mention that they were having marital problems?"

I hadn't anticipated how much this question would hit a nerve. Tabitha exploded at me quite unexpectedly.

"What are you trying to get at?" she yelled. "I don't know anything about Belinda. I've never met the woman in my life. Why are you here, anyway? To bring me pie and make me feel better, or to interrogate me? You know what, forget it. I should have known better than to think that anyone in Sunshine Springs actually cared about me!"

I took a step backward. I hadn't anticipated such a strong reaction, and the fire in Tabitha's eyes was scaring me. Remembering what I'd told myself about how it wasn't wise to come snooping around the house of a possible murderer, I decided that whatever I might learn about Belinda wasn't worth the danger I was putting myself in. Outside the front door, Sprinkles had started barking and scratching, trying to get in. But Tabitha had shut the door firmly, which meant my Dalmatian couldn't come to my rescue if I needed help.

"I'm sorry," I said, taking another step backward. "I didn't know that talking about Belinda would be so upsetting for you. I won't bother you further. Please, enjoy your pie. I'll get going now."

But Tabitha shrieked as I turned to leave.

"Oh no," she yelled. "You stop right there! You're not going anywhere."

I looked over my shoulder to make another quick apology before continuing my exit, but when I saw Tabitha, I froze.

She was standing behind the island, her face nearly purple with rage. In her hands, she held a gun.

A gun that was pointed straight at me.

Chapter Fourteen

The next thing I knew, I was blinking my eyes open in a daze. The world seemed to swim before me, like I was looking at it from underwater. It took me a few moments to remember where I was, but when Edgar Bates' kitchen came into focus, a feeling of dread filled me. Everything came rushing back. I remembered Tabitha shrieking at me and pointing a gun in my direction, and I remembered thinking that I was going to die. But everything after that was fuzzy.

What had happened? Had Tabitha actually shot me?

In a sudden panic, I took an inventory of my body. All of my limbs were intact, and I didn't see blood anywhere. Nothing felt particularly painful except for a large bump on my head which, as annoying as it was, was clearly not the result of a gunshot wound. It felt more like someone had whacked me in the head with something hard.

As everything began to come more and more into focus, I heard voices shouting in the distance. My heart leapt when I realized that those voices sounded like they belonged to Molly and Theo. I wasn't sure where Tabitha was, or how much danger I might still be in. But if Molly and Theo were here, then my chances of survival were much higher.

I struggled to sit up straighter, looking warily around me as I did. I had no idea where Tabitha was. For all I knew, she was still hiding just around the corner, waiting to take me out. But after sweeping my gaze across the whole room—at least the parts of the room I could see from where I sat—I didn't see anyone else. What I did see were signs of a struggle. Everywhere I looked, things were in a state of complete disarray. The box of Tabitha's photographs had been knocked over once again, and the photos were spread all over the kitchen. What was left of the pie that I had brought her had been tossed onto the floor in a smeary mess. Several of the other boxes that Tabitha had been packing up were also knocked over, and the room was filled with dishes, kitchen towels, and other items that had been scattered in the midst of some sort of apparent struggle. But where was Tabitha?

I heard the sound of Theo and Molly yelling once again, and this time, the sound was followed moments later by the sound of screeching tires and a car speeding away. My heart sank. Were they leaving me? Did they even know I was in the house? The thought that they might unknowingly be leaving me behind with Tabitha caused me to panic. I tried to call out to them, wherever they might be, but my voice sounded thick and gravelly, without much volume. Not that it mattered. If they had gotten in a car, they wouldn't be able to hear me. But I wasn't exactly thinking rationally at the moment. All I knew was that I was terrified of being left here alone with some crazy blonde in high heels who was wielding a gun around.

I needn't have worried. A few moments later, Molly and Theo came rushing into the kitchen. They were both talking at once in excited, anxious voices, but my fuzzy brain couldn't make out the words. It didn't matter what they were saying, though. I had never been so happy to see anyone in my life. To make things even better, I heard a loud bark, and realized that Sprinkles was coming in with them.

"Sprinkles," I said weakly. My Dalmatian ran over to me and greeted me with such enthusiasm that I was knocked backward onto the floor once again. I didn't care. I'd never been so happy to see that dog in my life.

Sprinkles wasn't the only one happy to see me. A moment later, Molly was on the floor beside me, hug-attacking me with just as much gusto.

"Thank heavens you're all right," she said as she squeezed me into a hug so tight I could barely breathe. "I was so worried that we'd lost you."

As happy as I was to see them, I realized that I still didn't know where Tabitha was. Did they know she was here and wandering around with a gun? I had to warn them!

"Tabitha," I sputtered out. "She has a gun!"

"She's not here anymore," Theo said. The calmness and strength in his voice unraveled me, and I felt like I might burst into tears of relief right then and there.

"Did you see her?" I asked, hoping that they had and that they were about to tell me that she was tied up somewhere, unable to cause further harm.

"We saw her," Molly said. "She was running out of the house like a madwoman, carrying a small box. When she saw us, she shrieked at us and told us to get away or that she was going to shoot us. She had a gun in one hand, but she wasn't holding it very steady. We asked her if you were here, and she yelled at us that she didn't know anything about you and that even if she did she wouldn't help us. I was afraid to press her too much on things because she was waving the gun around like crazy."

"She kept threatening to shoot us," Theo added. "But I'm not sure if she actually would have. She seemed really disoriented."

"Yeah," Molly agreed. "It was almost like she was out of her mind. Before Theo or I could figure out what else to do, she had jumped into her car. She threw the box and the gun on the passenger seat and sped out of here like we were the ones holding the gun. What in the world happened?"

Molly looked around at the mess of a room. I shook my head in an "I don't know" sort of way, then winced when I realized that that movement sent a sharp jab of pain running across my forehead.

"I'm not sure what happened. Like I texted you, I came over here to bring her pie and try to talk to her. She seemed to be relatively receptive to speaking with me until I accidentally knocked over this box of photos."

Molly and Theo glanced at the photos as I pointed at them, and seemed to be noticing them for the first time.

"Whoa!" Theo said. "Are those of Tabitha?"

I nodded, forgetting that the movement would cause me pain. I winced, and then continued explaining.

"Apparently, Tabitha had been doing some modeling. She claims that Edgar knew about it and thought it was cool that he was dating someone so wanted for her body. I'm not sure how true that was though, because she seemed quite distraught at the fact that I had seen the pictures. She definitely didn't seem proud of them. I decided it was best to change the subject, so I asked her about Belinda. I thought that would be a safe thing to talk about, but I was wrong. As soon as I mentioned Belinda, Tabitha started freaking out even more. The next thing I knew, she was pulling a gun on me. I don't remember much after that. I was sure I was dead at that point, but obviously I somehow made it out of all of this alive. Did you guys come in here and fight with her?"

"No," Molly said. "We'd just arrived when Tabitha came running out the front door. We weren't even sure if you were in here. You must have fought with her."

I laughed at the very idea. "I have no idea how to fight."

"Looks like you figured it out," Theo said. "Although it looks like you also got a nice goose egg on your forehead as a souvenir from your first fistfight."

I reached up and gingerly touched my forehead. "But I don't know how to fight," I said again, still confused.

Molly chuckled. "I would imagine that having a gun pointed in your face was pretty good motivation to try. You must have lunged at Tabitha or something, and the two of you went tumbling across this kitchen. It doesn't look like you left a single box unturned. She must have managed to sock you in the forehead at some point and knock you out. Then, luckily for you, she decided she'd rather escape than shoot you. My guess is that she went and grabbed a box of valuables and made a break for it before the police could get here."

The mention of police made me worry.

"Oh no!" I exclaimed. "You guys didn't call the police, did you?"

Theo raised an eyebrow at me. "Not yet. We haven't had time. But wouldn't you be eager for someone to call the police if you were in a situation where someone was holding a gun to your head?"

I gave him a sheepish look. "Yes, but as I'm sure you've realized by now, I'm trying to investigate Edgar's murder. You know Mitch is going to freak out when he realizes that."

Theo frowned at me. He was pretty good friends with Mitch, and it wouldn't surprise me if he went to tell Mitch that he'd caught me looking into the murder. My only saving grace was that Theo also wanted to stay on my good side, and he knew that tattling to Mitch was definitely going to put him on my bad side.

"I admire your bravery," Theo said with a shake of his head. "But I have to say that I think Mitch is right. You shouldn't be chasing after murderers. Look what happened tonight! You could have been killed."

"But I wasn't," I said brightly, forcing a smile onto my face.

Theo rolled his eyes at me, choosing not to even dignify that with a spoken response.

"How did you guys know I needed help, anyway? I know I texted Molly, but nothing in the text would have sounded overly alarming."

"It was Sprinkles," Molly said. "He must have heard you fighting with Tabitha. He knew you needed help, but he couldn't get in through the closed door. So he went running all the way down to the Sunshine Springs Winery."

My eyes widened. "But the winery must be at least three miles from here."

Molly shrugged. "That wasn't too great a distance for Sprinkles to run to save you. He ran straight up to Theo's villa and started barking at the front door. Theo came out, and when he saw Sprinkles barking like that all by himself, he knew you were in trouble. He called me right away, hoping that I might have an idea of where you were. Luckily, since you'd sent me that text, I knew to look for you here. Theo and I both rushed over and arrived just in time to see Tabitha making her escape."

I looked down at Sprinkles with tears in my eyes. His warm body was pressed against mine, as though he was afraid to lose contact with me for even a second.

"You really are a good dog," I said, my voice breaking a bit as I spoke. He looked up at my face and I wrapped my arms around him to nuzzle him close. Then I looked up at Theo and Molly. "And you two are good friends. Thanks for coming to get me."

"Of course," Molly said. "What else would we have done? You're my best friend. I don't know what I would do if I lost you. Seriously, could you be a bit more careful in the future?"

"I'll try," I said in a small voice.

Molly just sighed. We both knew that I would never be able to keep my curious side in check when there was a crime to be solved.

Theo shook his head at me, his expression a mixture of amusement, annoyance, and awe. He reached a hand down to me.

"Come on. Let's at least get you some fresh air. It would do you good. Once we're outside we can discuss calling the police. You know they're eventually going to find out about this. Might as well tell them sooner rather than later. As angry as Mitch is going to be at you for sticking your nose in all of this, he'll want to know that Tabitha pointed a gun at you. The fact that she has a gun might be evidence that she was the one who shot Edgar."

I gripped Theo's hand as he pulled me up, finding comfort in how warm and strong it was. I tried not to let myself think about the fact that Theo would be willing to let me hold that hand whenever I wanted to, if only I agreed to date him. Now was not the time to think about things like that. Now was the time to think about how to handle talking to Mitch about what had happened tonight.

I wasn't convinced that Tabitha's gun proved anything. We hadn't even established yet that the gun Tabitha had was the same kind as the gun that had been used to shoot Edgar. I suppose Mitch would want to look into that, although I had no idea what kind of gun Tabitha had been holding. Maybe Theo had been able to recognize it better. I didn't know the first thing about guns.

What I *did* know was that Tabitha didn't seem to know the first thing about guns either. Had the same woman who had been swinging that gun around like crazy tonight been the person who had taken steady aim from a faraway hiding place and shot Edgar? I supposed it was possible, but it didn't seem probable.

I didn't like the feeling of unease and uncertainty that filled me. Thankfully, Theo had been right about the fresh air. It felt soothing. As we stepped out onto the front porch, I took several deep breaths and instantly felt better. Even the throbbing in my forehead seemed to disappear.

I told myself there was no need to feel uneasy right now. I had been through an ordeal tonight, but at least I was alright now. I was alive and well other than a small bump on my head, I had my beloved dog by my side, and two of my best friends were here to make sure I stayed safe. On the whole, I had a lot to be thankful for. The fact that I still didn't know exactly who had killed Edgar wasn't the most important thing at the moment, and I should take a second to be grateful.

I took another deep breath, and gave Molly and Theo a wide smile. Theo seemed encouraged by this.

"That's it," he said gently. "Just relax, and everything's going to be alright."

This seemed like solid advice, and I had every intention of following it. But my best intentions flew out the window when I looked over in the bushes and saw a bright flash of orange. I did a double take, and looked again.

"Did you see that?" I asked.

"See what?" Molly and Theo both asked in unison.

"There, in the bushes. I saw a flash of orange. Someone's over there."

Molly and Theo both squinted and peered over at the bushes, which were only lit by moonlight right now.

"I don't see anything," Molly said.

"Neither do I," Theo agreed.

I chewed my lower lip and kept watching. I knew I had seen something. A moment later, I saw it again: the faintest flash of orange. It was so bright that the soft moonlight was enough for me to see it.

"There! There it was again!" I yelled.

And then, without waiting for Molly or Theo to tell me if they could see it too, I took off running toward the bushes. Theo shouted after me, yelling something about the fact that I might have a concussion and shouldn't be running. I ignored him. Whoever had broken into Edgar Bates' house was back.

This time, they weren't getting away.

Chapter Fifteen

My head instantly started throbbing again as I ran across the yard, but I ignored the pain. I had to know who was here. If it was Peter, I already knew that I could outrun him. Let's see what his excuse was when he got caught red-handed trying to sneak into his father's house.

Behind me, I could hear Theo and Molly following. Theo was still yelling at me that this was a bad idea, and Molly was simply begging me to stop. I ignored them both.

I didn't care if I had a concussion. I'd deal with that later. Right now, I needed to catch a murderer.

A moment later, I heard an excited bark. I looked down to my left just in time to see Sprinkles shooting past me, and I laughed. Whoever was running didn't stand a chance. Maybe they had enough of a head start to outrun me, but there was no way they were outrunning Sprinkles.

Sprinkles crashed through the bushes ahead of me and came out on the other side into an open, grassy area. His black-and-white spotted coat gleamed as he raced across the small field. He looked like poetry in motion, and I admired him for a moment before turning my attention back to the fleeing figure we were chasing. That's when I realized that we were chasing a woman, not a man. Behind me, Molly had just come crashing through the bushes and had realized the same thing.

"It's Belinda!" Molly said.

Indeed it was. I couldn't see her face, but the woman running away was the same height and build as Belinda, and that orange scarf she wore was a dead giveaway.

"Belinda, wait!" I shouted. "We just want to talk to you."

She didn't slow down, or even turn around. Why would she? If I had been trying to break into a house, I wouldn't be too keen on stopping to talk about it, either. Still, I was hopeful that Sprinkles would catch her. He was quickly gaining on her, his paws a blur as they raced across the grass.

But unfortunately for Sprinkles, and for me, Belinda had parked her car right on the road at the other end of the grassy field. She reached her car a good half-minute before Sprinkles did, giving her plenty of time to unlock it, climb in, and speed away.

For a few moments, my determined dog continued to chase her, even though it was hopeless. He went bounding down the street after her, barking as loudly as he could. But it was no use. His speedy legs were still no match for the engine of an automobile. Eventually, he gave up and turned to head back toward me with a defeated look on his face.

"It's okay, Sprinkles," I said, giving him a reassuring pat on the head. "You did your best."

A few seconds later, Theo and Molly both caught up with me at the same time.

"Are you out of your mind?" Theo asked, panting as he slowed to a stop.

I shrugged. "It's a good possibility. I've never claimed to be sane."

Theo did not look amused by my little joke. "What in the world are you doing, running around when you've just been hit on the head? And who was that, anyway?"

"That was Belinda Simmons," Molly said. "I'd bet my house on it."

Theo looked confused. "Belinda Simmons? What was she doing sneaking around in the bushes by Edgar Bates' house?"

"That's a very good question," I said. "And one I'm determined to get the answer to."

Theo looked exasperated. He'd clearly had enough. "Okay, I don't know what's going on here, but what I do know is that you shouldn't be running around. You need to go home and rest. I'd prefer it if you went and got your head looked at, but I have a feeling that you're going to refuse medical attention."

"That feeling is right," I said, crossing my arms. I didn't want to waste time right now having a paramedic look over me.

"Fine," Theo said. "I won't insist that you go see a doctor if you promise me that you're going to go home and rest. No more running around, and no more trying to catch burglars and murderers. In fact, you shouldn't even be driving. I'll drive you home. That way I know you get home safely, and I know you're not still running around after promising me that you won't."

"You're not the boss of me," I said in what was an admittedly juvenile tone of voice. But I didn't care how ridiculous I sounded. It was true. Theo couldn't tell me what to do. Maybe that macho boss mentality worked on his winery employees, because he actually was their boss. But it wasn't going to work on me. I crossed my arms and resisted the urge to stick my tongue out at him. Before our petty argument could devolve any further, Molly stepped in.

"I can take Izzy home," she said. Then she turned to look at me. "You know Theo is right. You should rest. And besides, Belinda is long gone. There's no way we can catch up with her now, and I'm sure she's not going to be back here tonight. Not when she knows that someone saw her trying to sneak in."

Still, I hesitated. Theo let out another exasperated sigh, and reached over to put a hand on my shoulder. I hated to admit how comforting his touch was, and I scowled at him so that he wouldn't have any indication that I might actually be enjoying the friendly gesture.

"You need to take care of yourself, Izzy," he said in a firm but caring voice. "I'm going to insist that you do. Here are your choices: you can either go home with Molly right now and rest, or you can stay here with me while I call Mitch and tell him everything that's happened. I'm sure you'd love to be here when he arrives so that you can answer all his questions. You know he's going to have a lot of them."

My shoulders slumped. Theo had me there. There was no way I wanted to talk to Mitch tonight. As it was, I was sure Sheriff Mitch would be knocking on my café door first thing in the morning to ask for a statement. But given the choice of dealing with it now or dealing with it in the morning, I'd rather choose the morning. At least then I could rush him along and tell him I had too much to do in my pie shop to spend a long time talking to him.

"Fine, I'll go home with Molly. But you have to promise me that you won't tell Mitch I was investigating the murder."

"I'll tell him as little as possible," Theo said. "But I have to tell him you were here. I can't exactly report the whole incident and not mention that you were at the center of it."

"Fine, whatever. Just try to downplay as much as possible the fact that I was here to interrogate Tabitha."

"I will, if you get out of here now," Theo said, making a shooing motion in the direction of Edgar's house.

Without another word, I followed Molly and him back through the bushes. I climbed into Molly's little red sports car, and gave Theo my car keys. He promised me that he'd have one of the police officers drive it over to my place later that night, and I bid him goodbye, trying not to sound too annoyed with him.

He had come to my rescue, after all. And I knew he was genuinely concerned for my well-being. Still, it annoyed me that he thought he could boss me around. If I wanted to go around sleuthing tonight, what business was it of his?

Sprinkles climbed into Molly's car as well, hopping into the middle of the backseat. He stuck his head into the front, looking back and forth between Molly and me, and giving each of us a wet, sloppy kiss.

Molly laughed. "Sprinkles! Get out of my face so I can drive."

Sprinkles let out a joyous woof, but he did back off a bit. I looked past him and grinned mischievously at Molly as she started pulling out of the driveway.

"Do you know where Belinda lives?" I asked.

Molly gave me a sharp look. "No, Izzy. Theo is right. You need to get home."

"You know me better than that," I said. "There's no way I'm going to be able to go home and sleep with everything that happened tonight spinning through my mind. I want to go confront Belinda. She knows something, and I'm going to find out what it is. You can come with me now, or you can drop me off at home. Then as soon as one of the police officers brings my car back, I'm going to go over to Belinda's by myself. No one can stop me."

Molly glared at me. "Why are you so ridiculously stubborn?"

I grinned at her. "I get it from Grams."

Molly groaned. "That's the truth, although your grandmother would be upset with you if she knew you might have a concussion and were still going to go confront a possible murderer in the middle of the night."

"I don't have a concussion. Theo was overreacting. And it's not the middle of the night. It's not even ten o'clock yet."

"That's still late enough that you shouldn't be showing up unannounced at people's houses. But I know that you're not going to stop and rest until you have a chance to talk to Belinda, and I would rather you didn't go alone."

"So you'll take me?"

"I'll take you," Molly agreed reluctantly. "But only if you swear to me that after we go to Belinda's house you'll let me take you home—and you'll actually lie down and rest. You have to keep that promise, too. You already promised Theo you'd go rest, and you clearly have no intention of doing so. Theo is one thing, but you better not make false promises to me."

I shrugged. "What he doesn't know can't hurt him, right?"

Molly let out another long, exasperated sigh. "Probably not. Come on. Let's get this over with so I can get you home to rest."

I knew Molly wasn't happy with me, but she'd get over it eventually. Besides, I knew she was excited to be involved in my sleuthing efforts. Part of the reason she had agreed to take me to Belinda's was because she didn't want to be left out when I did go. She wanted to know what I would find when I confronted Belinda. I had a feeling I was on the verge of a big breakthrough in this case, and I knew Molly had that same feeling. She wanted to see what that breakthrough would be.

I could hardly keep from bouncing in my seat with excitement as Molly started driving to Belinda Simmons' house.

Chapter Sixteen

Fifteen minutes later, we pulled onto Belinda's street. Molly killed her headlights and slowed to a crawl so that there wouldn't be enough light and noise to alert Belinda that we were coming.

I wasn't sure that I dared to hope that she was actually there. If I'd just been caught trying to break into a house, I'm not sure I would have gone straight home. I might have been afraid that that's exactly where someone would come looking for me. Of course, maybe going home and acting like you'd been home the whole time was the best thing to do. I could only hope that Belinda had returned here to try to innocently act like she'd been here the whole time. Surely, she couldn't stay away too long. Frank would get suspicious.

To my relief, when we pulled up in front of Belinda's house, the same car that Belinda had used to escape from Edgar Bates' house was now parked in her driveway.

"She's here," I said excitedly.

"She is," Molly murmured. "That's her car. But that other car isn't Frank's. I don't know who it belongs to. It doesn't look like the car of any local."

I considered this information. If the car wasn't Frank's, that might mean that the Simmons had visitors. Did we really want to confront Belinda about all of this when some random person was in the house?

I wasn't sure, and neither was Molly. She continued driving past the house to park a few houses down on the street. We didn't want to be right in front of Belinda's house where she would see us if she looked out the window. I didn't know if she'd been able to see that Molly and I had been the ones chasing her earlier, and I wasn't sure if she'd recognize Molly's car. Better to be on the safe side and not park in a glaringly obvious spot. Once Molly felt we were at a safe distance, she killed the engine. Molly, Sprinkles and I all turned around to look out the rearview window. Belinda's house looked dark and quiet.

"What do you think?" Molly asked. "Should we try to knock on the front door? Or is it not a good idea since we don't know who might be in there?"

Molly didn't say it out loud, but I had a feeling that she was thinking the same thing I was: did the strange car in front of Belinda's house belong to someone dangerous? If Belinda was a murderer, she might hang out with some questionable characters. Were we getting in over our heads by trying to take this case into our own hands?

I'd already been threatened at gunpoint once tonight. Wasn't that enough? I didn't want to add any more bumps to my head, and I certainly didn't want to risk another close encounter with bullets.

But before I could make a decision or express any of my concerns to Molly, the front door of Belinda's house suddenly opened. Molly and I glanced at each other with worried, curious faces, and then glanced back at the house. Had Belinda seen us driving by even though we'd attempted to be stealthy?

But then, we saw a tall man stepping out onto the porch. Belinda didn't turn her porch light on, but the moonlight was enough for me to see that he wasn't anyone I knew.

"Who is that?" I whispered to Molly, as though if I talked any louder the man might hear me even though I was inside a car and several houses away.

Molly shook her head. "I don't know. I've never seen him before. I'm sure he's not a local."

I felt a chill run through me. Who was this man, and why was Belinda hanging out with him? Was he someone who had assisted in the murder of Edgar Bates? After the night I'd had, anything seemed possible. Molly must have had similar thoughts.

"Maybe we should get out of here while we still can," she said. "That man might be dangerous."

I was about to agree with Molly when the man suddenly stepped toward Belinda, wrapped his arms around her, and planted a long, deep kiss on her mouth. My jaw dropped as I watched Belinda wrap her arms around the man and kiss him back, then hurriedly pull away.

She looked nervously around as though worried someone might be watching, and she had reason to worry. Sunshine Springs was a gossip-hungry town, and the fact that Belinda Simmons had just kissed a man who was not her husband would be prime gossip for anyone who saw.

For a few terrifying moments, I thought she would notice Molly's car. But she overlooked the car, probably thinking it wasn't worth noticing when it was turned off and dark. She didn't realize that Molly and I were sitting inside that car gawking at her.

When the man tried to kiss her again, Belinda gave him a little push toward his car. She shook her head as she looked nervously around once more. I was sure she was telling him that they'd already done too much in plain view. The man seemed to accept this because he nodded, gave her a small wave, and made his way to his car. He got in and drove away as Belinda disappeared into her house once more.

Molly and I looked at each other in a state of shock. This had not been what we'd expected at all.

"Where's Frank?" I finally managed to stammer out.

"Not here. That's for sure," Molly said. "No wonder Belinda's been sneaking around so much, and no wonder she and Frank have been having issues. Looks like she found herself something on the side."

"Looks that way," I agreed. "But that still doesn't explain why she was sneaking around Edgar Bates' house. There's a whole lot of strange going on here, if you ask me."

"I agree," Molly said. "What do you say we go ask Belinda about it?"

I smiled. "I'd say that's a very good idea."

Now that I knew that the stranger was just some lover of Belinda's and not a criminal accomplice of some sort, I felt more confident about confronting her. I also felt that we now had some leverage to get her to talk. If we told her that we'd seen her kissing a man that wasn't Frank, she would probably be desperate for a way to convince us to stay silent. I was willing to consider silence in exchange for information on what she knew about Edgar Bates.

Molly, Sprinkles, and I all got out of the car and made our way toward Belinda's front door. Time to see if we could get Belinda to play ball with us.

Chapter Seventeen

Several knocks on Belinda's door yielded nothing but silence. Either Belinda had escaped out the back door, or she was determined to act like she wasn't there. My guess was she was hiding in her house. She couldn't get to her car without us seeing her, so if she did leave, she would have been limited to places she could get to on foot. After a few rounds of knocking and ringing the doorbell with no results, I decided to make her an offer she couldn't refuse.

"I know you're in there, Belinda," I yelled. "And unless you come talk to us, I'm going to tell everyone in town about the man I just saw you kissing on your porch."

That did the trick. A few moments later, I heard the deadbolt unlatching from the inside, and then the front door flew open. Belinda stood there, still wearing her orange scarf and looking both angry and panicked at the same time.

"Fine!" she hissed. "Come in. Just stop yelling about Tom loud enough for the neighbors to hear."

I didn't bother telling her that it was only a matter of time before everyone in town knew about this Tom guy, no matter how quiet I was about it. If she was getting careless enough to kiss him on her front doorstep, even in the darkness, then she was bound to have someone spot her sooner rather than later. But that wasn't my problem, and right now, the fact that she wanted to keep things quiet worked in my favor.

"The dog stays outside," Belinda snapped as Sprinkles tried to follow me inside. I gave Sprinkles an apologetic look, and he sat down forlornly outside the front door. He was getting used to being told to wait outside when I was sleuthing around, but that didn't mean he didn't act annoyed about it. I always gave him extra pie to make up for the times he was excluded.

"Where's Frank?" Molly asked as we walked into the house. She looked around as though Frank might magically appear, even though it was obvious he wasn't there. There was no way Belinda would have had Tom in the house at the same time as Frank.

"Frank is out of town," Belinda said. "He took a job a few cities over to remodel the mansion of some fancy-pants winery owner. Apparently, before Edgar was shot, he'd recommended Frank for the job. Frank doesn't normally like to work outside of Sunshine Springs, but the guy insisted and was willing to pay so much that Frank would have been stupid to refuse."

"And you would have been stupid not to take advantage of Frank's time away to see your lover?" Molly asked.

Belinda glared at her. "Look, I'm not proud of the fact that I've been sneaking around on Frank. But I've been really unhappy for a really long time. He's just gotten so old and boring. All he cares about is work, work, work. I complained that he wasn't spontaneous enough, and the best he could do was buy me this orange scarf. Now I have to wear it all the time to act like I actually like it. It's not that I want to break his heart or hurt his feelings. It's just that I want more from life than just living for the next remodel job."

"Is that why you were breaking into Edgar Bates' house tonight?" I asked. "Looking for a little excitement?"

Belinda turned her glare in my direction. "I don't know what you're talking about."

I rolled my eyes. "Don't try to play dumb, Belinda. I saw you running away. Molly saw you too, and so did Theo."

Belinda looked alarmed. "Theo?"

"Yes, Theo," Molly said. "He was with us at Edgar Bates' house, and we all saw you running away. There's no use trying to deny it. If you know what's good for you, you'll explain why you were breaking into Edgar's house before we're forced to tell the whole town about Tom."

Belinda's face turned pale.

"I wasn't there," she tried to insist one more time.

Molly and I just stared at her with skeptical looks on our faces. Finally, she gave in.

"Okay, fine!" she said as she buried her face in her hands. "I was there. But it's not what you think. I wasn't trying to steal anything from Edgar. Nothing of real value, at least."

"Then what were you doing there?" I demanded. "I have to say, I'm beginning to get awfully suspicious of you in this whole murder investigation. You were sneaking around right before Edgar died at the party. Now you've been acting strangely according to everyone in town, which I guess could be because you've been sneaking around on Frank. But it also could be because you're somehow involved with what happened to Edgar. Why were you at his house, and why did Tabitha freak out when I asked her about you?"

Belinda's face paled. "You asked Tabitha about me? What did she say?"

"Nothing good, that's for sure," I said. "In fact, asking her about you is how I ended up with this giant goose egg on my forehead."

I pointed to the tender spot on my forehead and Belinda winced.

"Wow, she got you good."

I threw my hands up in frustration. "Yes, she did. But why? Why was she so upset when I mentioned you?"

Belinda hesitated a moment, unsure of whether she wanted to answer that question. Finally, she sighed in resignation and started speaking.

"Tabitha doesn't like me very much. I went over to Edgar's house a few times while Frank was remodeling the kitchen there, and every time she made it clear that I wasn't welcome."

"Interesting," I said. "Tabitha claims she never met you."

Belinda laughed. "She probably wishes she'd never met me, and the feeling is mutual. I wish I'd never met her."

"Why's that?"

"Getting tangled up with her has been nothing but a headache. While I was over there one day, I found out some things about Tabitha that she didn't want me to know."

"Let me guess," I said. "You found out that she does some, shall we say, *modeling* on the side."

Belinda looked over at me in surprise. "How do you know about that?"

96

"I was over there talking to her today and a box of her pictures got knocked over. She tried to act nonchalant about it, but I could tell she was rattled."

Belinda gave a dry little laugh. "I'm sure she was rattled. She apparently makes quite a bit of money on the side from those photographs. I guess a modeling career nets you a lot of money when you model with almost no clothes on. But she knew Edgar would be insanely jealous if he knew anyone else was seeing her like that, so she had to hide the pictures from him."

"So he didn't know about them? Tabitha claimed that he did know, and even liked the pictures."

Belinda shook her head. "No way. Edgar didn't like to share. Tabitha was worried that if he discovered those photos, he would flip his lid and kick her out of the house. Luckily for her, hiding things from a hundred-year-old man isn't that difficult. All she had to do was put her boxes of photos and anything related to them up on a high shelf. It's not like Edgar was climbing up any stepladders."

Understanding dawned on me. "But one day you somehow found out about the photos."

Belinda nodded. "I was looking on one of the top shelves in Edgar's garage for some tools for Frank. He often leaves tools and supplies at a jobsite when he's doing a lengthy remodel, and I was helping him pull down some supplies he needed that day."

"Were you over there often, then?"

Belinda shrugged. "Maybe once or twice a week. I didn't love the place, but Frank was really into that job. He was hanging out with Edgar a lot, and this was before I met Tom. I didn't have much to fill my time when Frank was gone, so I was over there a decent amount when I wasn't working myself."

"I can't believe Tabitha said she'd never met you," Molly piped in.

"Well, like I said," Belinda replied. "She probably wishes she'd never met me. We didn't get along from the start, and when I saw those photos I couldn't resist confronting her with them. Now I wish I'd just kept my mouth shut. I didn't realize how much I was poking a hornet's nest. But I didn't like her, and I knew she didn't want Edgar to see those photos. I decided to use the photos as leverage. I admit it was a little petty, but any time she annoyed me I would threaten to tell Edgar about the photos. That worked well for a while, until I started dating Tom."

"Uh-oh," I said. I could already see where this was going.

"Long story short," Belinda said, "Tabitha had been stalking me and I didn't realize it. She'd been looking for some dirt on me, so that she could threaten me right back when I threatened her. Until Tom, there really wasn't anything scandalous about my life. But because she'd been stalking me, Tabitha knew as soon as Tom entered the scene. She immediately let me know she knew, and threatened to tell Frank about Tom if I told Edgar about the pictures."

"Okay," Molly said slowly. "So the scales were even at that point. But now that Edgar's dead, what motivation does Tabitha have to keep quiet if she wanted to cause trouble for you?"

"Tabitha has practically made a career out of being a gold digger," Belinda answered. "The modeling is just what gets her through between men. She bounces around from old man to old man, trying to convince them to name her in their wills. So far, she's been unsuccessful at that, and hasn't managed to snag any inheritance money. I imagine she was quite disappointed at the fact that Edgar left her nothing. I think she really thought that he was the one who would finally leave her a fortune and set her up for life."

I couldn't resist a chuckle. "She got that wrong."

Belinda nodded. "Tabitha got nothing, as you know. That means she has to find another old man. Since all these old rich guys don't seem to like dating a woman who poses for almost nude photos, Tabitha keeps that side of her life quiet. She needs that modeling money to survive in between living at an old man's house and mooching off of him. If it were to become common knowledge that she was doing these kinds of photos, her method of jumping from old man boyfriend to old man boyfriend wouldn't work anymore."

Molly and I both stared at Belinda with looks of shock on our faces.

"She sort of sounds like a sleaze," Molly finally said.

Belinda shrugged. "I'm not sure I'm in a position to judge other people's dating choices. But anyway, not long before the big hundredth birthday party, Edgar found out about Tom. At first, I assumed he'd found out from Tabitha."

"A logical assumption," I said.

"Yes," Belinda agreed. "But when I went to Tabitha in a rage to tell her that I was going to tell Edgar about her photos, she once again threatened to tell Edgar about Tom in retribution. She didn't seem to know that Edgar already knew about Tom, which implied that Edgar had learned of my infidelity to Frank some other way. But I was angry, and decided Tabitha must be faking her apparent surprise. I went to Edgar and told him about the photos, expecting him to immediately blow up at Tabitha."

"But he didn't?" Molly guessed.

"He didn't," Belinda confirmed. "He also didn't immediately tell Frank that I was cheating on him. Instead, Edgar decided he wanted to do something much more dramatic."

"He did have a flair for the dramatic," I said, thinking about how Edgar had requested that his will be read aloud to the entire town.

"He did," Belinda agreed. "And this time, he had something especially dramatic planned. He told me that he knew a lot of the secrets of people in this town, and that over his hundred years of life he'd grown sick of secrets. He'd decided that he was going to give a speech at his hundredth birthday party revealing the secrets of many of the townspeople."

Suddenly, Peter's reluctance to let his father read that speech made perfect sense. Peter must have known what was in the speech, and he hadn't wanted his father's birthday party to turn into a circus. He also hadn't wanted his father's funeral to turn into a circus.

"Do you have any idea what exactly was in the speech?" I asked. "Or whether anyone else knew that Edgar was planning to reveal a bunch of secrets?"

"The only thing that I know for sure was in there was something about the fact that I was cheating on Frank, and something about Tabitha's modeling. I do know there was more than that, but I don't know what it was. I tried to get Edgar to talk to me about it, but he wouldn't say a word. He wanted to keep all of the secrets for himself until the big reveal."

"Did Tabitha know that he was planning to do this?" Molly asked.

"I don't think so. Edgar would have enjoyed shocking her in front of everyone. She was so sure that she was going to get money from him that he probably thought it would be hilarious to tell her in front of everyone that he knew her secrets and she wasn't getting anything. Tabitha might have known that Edgar had a speech and that it was full of secrets, but I don't think she realized that Edgar had discovered her secret."

"I think that's right," Molly said excitedly. Then she turned to me. "Remember at Edgar's funeral? Peter claimed that he'd lost the speech, and Tabitha was angry and calling him incompetent. She wouldn't have been angry at him for losing the speech if she'd known that there were sordid details about her in there."

Belinda nodded. "I wasn't at Edgar's funeral, but that sounds about right. Tabitha probably thought that the speech was something detrimental to Peter, and that's why she wanted it read."

"Do you think there was something about Peter in the speech?" I asked.

Belinda shrugged. "Maybe, although I can't imagine what. Peter might be a bit of a jerk sometimes, but he doesn't seem to have anything scandalous in his life at all. All he does is work, work, work. But if there is anything scandalous to know about him, his father would be the one to know. And trust me: Edgar wasn't above outing his own son. He and Peter had a stormy relationship. They tolerated each other for the most part, but there were definitely some explosive fights between them."

"I bet there was something about Peter in there," Molly said. "That's why he was so determined not to have the speech read."

"Maybe," Belinda said. "Or maybe he just didn't want his dad to cause such a stir in the community. He was probably afraid that people would take it out on him and it would hurt his business."

I narrowed my eyes at Belinda. "And what about you? You didn't want the speech read either. Maybe you shot Edgar to keep him from ruining things between you and Frank."

Belinda laughed loudly. "Look, I may be an awful, cheating wife, but I'm not a murderer. I'm not going to kill someone just so that Frank doesn't find out that I'm running around on him. I'm planning to tell him myself, I just haven't worked up the guts to do it. I think our relationship is done and not worth saving, but I want to find a way to let him down gently. I actually intended to tell him before Edgar's party so that he wouldn't find out in front of the whole town. But I chickened out like a coward, and decided to make myself scarce while the speech was being read. I didn't want to face the truth in front of everyone or see the expression on Frank's face when he found out."

"Well, aren't you just a peach," Molly said sarcastically.

Belinda's cheeks turned pink. "Like I said, I'm not proud of it."

"Speaking of things you're not proud of," I said. "What were you doing breaking into Edgar's house? Trying to get a copy of the speech?"

"Yes. Can you blame me? Edgar kept the things that were most precious to him in his safe. I know that because he told Frank one day that he was worried about Tabitha taking a ring that was a family heirloom. He said he put the ring in the safe because that was the safest place in the house. I'm sure Edgar would have used the safe to store both paper copies of the speech as well as electronic storage devices that contained the speech."

"But Peter also has a copy of the speech," I pointed out.

Belinda nodded. "At the birthday party, Peter had convinced Edgar to let him hold the envelope that contained the speech. Edgar was reluctant to turn it over, but Peter made up some line about how the speech was going to end up with wine spilled on it. I happened to be standing right there when Edgar handed it over. After Edgar was shot, Peter was more than happy to keep that speech to himself. And if there was indeed something bad about Peter in there, I'm sure he destroyed the speech. Even if there wasn't anything about him specifically, Peter might have just wanted the speech gone. He doesn't share his father's fascination with revealing secrets."

I frowned. "But wouldn't Peter have suspected that there was another copy in the safe? Surely he knew that his father kept his most valuable possessions in the safe, and it sounds like this speech was quite important to Edgar."

"Peter might suspect that there's another copy in the safe," Belinda said. "But getting any copies from the safe would be difficult for Peter, because he doesn't have the combination. The only person besides Edgar who had the combination to the safe was Edgar's lawyer."

"Is there a chance the lawyer has any extra copies of the speech now?" Molly asked.

Belinda shook her head no. "I don't think Edgar's lawyer has been to the house yet, since Tabitha is still there. As for Peter, if he wanted to get into the safe then he'd have to break into the house and forcefully break the safe open. I know he's been to the house to try to convince Tabitha to let him in, but as far as I know she's been locking him out."

Molly furrowed her brow. "Is that why you were breaking into the house? To break into the safe?"

Belinda shrugged and nodded. "I figured it was worth a shot."

"Do you even know how to break into a safe?" I asked. I'd only seen safes broken into in the movies, and those safes were always insanely complicated.

"I could figure it out," Belinda said confidently. "Over the years I've picked up a lot of tricks from Frank on how to use various tools. I don't think Edgar's safe was particularly heavy duty, so given enough time and the right tools, I thought I could get into it."

"But you didn't have enough time, because you realized we were at Edgar's house."

"Exactly. Or, maybe it's better to say *you* realized *I* was there. I couldn't sneak past you quietly once you saw me and started chasing me. So I took off running and figured I'd have to come again and try another day."

I thought of the first time I'd visited Tabitha, and the fact that there'd been a burglar that day, too. "How many times have you tried to break in already?"

"This was the first time I tried."

I narrowed my eyes at Belinda again. "Don't lie to me. I saw you there a few days ago. You had the same orange scarf on."

Belinda looked genuinely confused. "I don't know what you're talking about. I only tried to break in for the first time tonight."

I kept glaring at her. Was she telling me the truth? She hadn't exactly impressed me with her morals at this point, so I was inclined to think she was lying to me. But I decided it didn't matter much how many times she'd tried to break in. The important thing here was that she'd told me what she was looking for. I wondered who else had secrets in that speech, and who else might have known about it. There might be quite a few people in this town who'd had a motive to murder Edgar Bates.

I wanted a copy of that speech. The only problem was that it sounded like the only way to get a copy was to break into Edgar's house and open his safe. I had no idea how to do that, and I doubted that Belinda would be excited to give me tips. I decided I'd learned all I could from her for the moment.

"Alright, thanks for your time. Molly and I should get going."

Molly looked relieved by this. I had a feeling she'd been ready to go since the moment we got here. But she'd forgive me for dragging her into this, because we'd found out some very interesting information while here.

Belinda, however, didn't look relieved. Belinda looked panicked. "You're not going to tell Frank about Tom, are you?"

I had almost forgotten about my threats to tell Frank. I didn't really care what happened between Belinda and Frank—that was for them to figure out. I'd only threatened to tell Frank so that I'd have leverage to get Belinda to talk.

"I won't say anything if you promise to stay away from Edgar's house." I thought about telling her that she had to help me get the speech, but then I thought that was probably going too far. I wasn't sure I trusted her enough to break into Edgar's house together and open the safe. Besides, Mitch would kill me if I broke into Edgar's house and cracked the safe open. The best thing to do here was to talk to Mitch and let him deal with the safe, even though I was reluctant to hand over the investigation.

For now, Belinda was nodding her head. "Fine. I shouldn't have tried that anyway. I need to just talk to Frank and come clean with him so that we can both move on with our lives. By the time that speech is found and possibly revealed to everyone in town, I'll have already talked to Frank."

"That sounds like a good idea," I said as I turned toward the door. "Secrets are nearly impossible to keep in this town, anyway."

"You'd think," Belinda said. "But I think there were a lot of secrets in that speech that had been kept pretty well. Edgar really wanted to make a scene, and if whoever finds that speech wants to make a scene as well, they'll have all the ammo they need to do so."

I muttered a noncommittal response and turned to leave. But as Molly and I walked back to her car with Sprinkles trailing behind us, I could only think about what else might be in Edgar's speech. Who else had secrets they didn't want revealed? And who else knew about Edgar's plan to reveal those secrets?

Had someone wanted to keep a secret badly enough that they would have shot Edgar to do so? That was the only reasonable explanation for his murder. The trouble now would be figuring out who had a secret so big that they would kill to keep it.

Chapter Eighteen

The next morning, Mitch stopped by the Drunken Pie Café bright and early to ask me questions about the night before. I had known he was coming, but having to talk to him still put me in a bad mood. He wanted to know why I had been at Edgar's house, and he wasn't buying my story that I had just gone to be nice to Tabitha.

"Come on, Izzy. Do you really think I'm that dumb? I know by now that when there's something to investigate, you're going to stick your nose into it. Why were you really over there?"

It would have been a good time to tell Mitch everything I knew. He would have been angry, but he was going to find out eventually, anyway. I couldn't keep what I'd learned about the case a secret for very long, and whether he found out now or later wasn't going to make much difference in how angry he was at me. Might as well rip off the Band-Aid and get it over with, especially since I was pretty sure that I would need his help if I wanted to get into the safe and see the speech.

But Mitch's snotty attitude rubbed me the wrong way, and I decided that I wasn't ready to tell him everything I knew just yet. I had a few more things I wanted to check before I turned this investigation completely over to him, so I stuck to my story. I insisted that I didn't know anything, and that I'd only been to see Tabitha because I wanted to be nice and take her pie.

Finally, Mitch gave up and left—but not before warning me that he knew I knew something, and that he was going to figure out a way to make me tell him. I breathed a sigh of relief as I watched him leave. I had no doubt that he would figure out a way to make me talk. In fact, I wanted to talk. Just not yet. It was a worry for another time.

Right now, I needed to get through the day at the pie shop. Then I could check on a few other things before figuring out how I was going to talk to Mitch and tell him about the speech that might be hiding in the safe. I wanted to tell him in a way that would ensure that he would keep me in the loop about what was going on. That wasn't going to be easy to do.

Mitch had already refused to tell me this morning whether Tabitha was still in town or whether she'd succeeded in making a break for it. He didn't want to give me any information if I wasn't going to admit that I was playing detective. That was okay. I would find out what I wanted to know a different way. Scott would hear the gossip and tell me, or if all else failed I'd go down to the Sunshine Springs Winery and convince Theo to talk to me. Theo didn't like telling me no, a fact that often worked to my advantage when I was trying to find out something that Mitch had told him.

Molly wasn't working with me today, and the pie shop was busy. Without anyone to help me serve customers, the day flew by in an exhausting blur. I had to answer about a thousand questions about what had happened to my face. The goose egg looked even worse today than it had the day before. I tried to cover it up with makeup as best I could, and that did make the bruise look better. But there was no hiding the swelling. It looked like I had a giant golf ball tucked under the skin of my forehead.

By the time closing time came, I was ready to go home and call it a day. But I already had plans to go with Molly to the park where Edgar's hundredth birthday party had been—plans I wasn't willing to cancel. We wanted to check out the bathroom and see whether it had a good vantage point onto the field where Edgar had been sitting during the fireworks. I wouldn't be able to stop thinking about the possibilities until I went to look at the bathroom myself.

As far as I could tell, Tabitha had been in the bathroom the whole time the fireworks were going on. The night of the party, I hadn't seen Tabitha coming back out of the bathrooms after she went in, and my spot at the food tables had been right by the bathrooms. I would have seen her if she'd come out.

That meant that if she had been the one to kill Edgar, she would have needed to be able to shoot from the bathroom's window. If the bathroom's windows didn't give a clear shot, then odds were that Tabitha wasn't the killer.

Molly arrived at the pie shop at six o'clock, just as she'd promised. She found me sitting at one of the café tables eating a slice of lemon vodka pie. Beside me, Sprinkles was eating a slice of key lime pie—his favorite. He'd been hiding out in the back room all day today, and he was excited to get pie and not be cooped up anymore. We'd take him with us to the park, and he'd be even more excited for the chance to run around there.

Molly raised an eyebrow at me as she walked across the café.

"You look exhausted. Maybe you should go home and rest and we can try again tomorrow. You had quite a night last night, after all. Have you seen a doctor yet?"

"I don't need to see a doctor," I insisted. "I'm fine. It's just a bump, not a concussion, and I don't want to wait until tomorrow to see what we can find out by looking at the park. I want to scout it out before talking to Mitch, and I can't hold him off much longer. He knows I know something, and besides, I shouldn't keep this from him. If that speech is in the safe and it does have a bunch of secrets, as Belinda seems to think, then maybe it will help Mitch figure out who was determined enough to protect their secrets that they killed Edgar to do so."

"Alright, if you really think you're up for it. But I want a slice of pie before we go. Do you have any death by chocolate left?"

"Sure do. You know where everything is. Help yourself."

About thirty minutes later, Molly and I were back at the park where Edgar had been shot. Sprinkles bounced excitedly around us as we stood in the same spot where the dessert tables had been on that fateful night. Now, there was only concrete and grass there, some of the grass still slightly trampled from where so many people had been walking through. The grassy lawn where Edgar had been shot stretched out in front of us. Today, of course, there were no picnic blankets or people there. Only the long field with a long sidewalk running around it that was occasionally lit by a streetlight.

"It looks so different with no people, doesn't it?" Molly asked.

"It does," I agreed. "And knowing that someone died on that field out there gives it a bit of an eerie feeling."

I shivered, and Molly nodded.

"Let's get this over with," she said.

We headed for the nearby park bathrooms where Tabitha had been the night of the party. The lights came on automatically as we

106

walked inside, dimly illuminating a small room made mostly of concrete. The mirror was covered with smudges and the floor was littered with a smattering of leaves and sticks from the outside, but otherwise the place was fairly clean. I peeked into the two stalls just to be sure that there wasn't a window in there. You wouldn't think that anyone would put a window in a stall itself, but I'd seen some strange things in public restrooms and I wanted to be sure. After determining that there was no window in the stalls, I turned to look at the one window that the bathroom did have. I peered out of it and Molly came to stand beside me and peer out as well.

The window looked directly out onto a giant tree trunk.

"There's no way anyone could have shot Edgar from here," Molly said, stating the obvious. I murmured my agreement. Tabitha would have had to have exited the bathroom and shot Edgar from somewhere outside. It would have been hard for her to sneak past Molly, Mitch, and me without us seeing her. We hadn't exactly been paying close attention to her that night, but all three of us remembered seeing her go in the bathroom but not coming out. We couldn't say with one hundred percent certainty that she'd been in here the whole time, but I would say odds were better than not.

Even if she had exited, she would have needed to stash the gun somewhere quickly. That wouldn't have been easy to do in the heels and dress she'd been wearing. Mitch had searched her car and all of the surrounding area, but the gun had never been found.

"I suppose it's still possible that she was the killer," I observed. "But it's looking more and more unlikely."

"What about Belinda?" Molly asked. "You said you saw her sneaking around right before the fireworks went off. Of course, she claims she didn't kill Edgar, but can we really believe her? She has the motive, because she wanted to keep things about her relationship with Tom quiet. And she could have gotten away. No one was looking for her, and no one really knows where she was after the shooting happened. Maybe she got in her car, drove away, and hid the gun before anyone had even realized exactly what had happened. It was so chaotic after the gunshot went off."

"I think you might be right," I said. "I don't think Tabitha knew about the fact that she was supposedly listed in that speech. And I just think she's not smart enough to pull off a shooting without getting caught."

"She's not coordinated enough, for that matter," Molly said. "She's always wobbling around on those heels, and wearing outfits that make me wonder how it's possible for her to even move."

"I know what you mean," I said with a chuckle. "Although, she did have a gun when you were at her house last night."

"True," Molly said. "But we don't know if it was the same gun that was used to shoot Edgar, and I just don't see how she could have hidden it somewhere without Mitch finding it the night of the murder."

Molly and I stood silently in the bathroom, contemplating all of this for a few moments.

"So, where do we go from here?" Molly eventually asked.

I sighed. "I suppose it's time to talk to Mitch. The only other thing I can think to do is to confront Peter and ask him about the speech. But since he pulled a knife on me the last time I talked to him, I'm not sure I want to try that again, especially now that I might have information he doesn't want everyone to know."

Molly grinned at me. "Why do you sound so dejected? You act like you just failed this investigation. You've done a great job, and even though Mitch will give you a hard time about it, he'll be glad to know what you've found out. He probably wouldn't have discovered all of that on his own. You've helped him out a lot, and I bet there will be something in the speech that will help Mitch figure out who actually killed Edgar."

"You're right," I said. "I just wish I would have actually figured out exactly who the killer was. But I think that's not going to be possible to do without getting the speech, and there's no way I'm going to be able to get that speech out of the safe."

"No," Molly said. "You definitely shouldn't try to do that. You shouldn't be breaking and entering. Tabitha might still be there, and you've seen that she's dangerous. And what if you run into Peter or Belinda? They might be willing to hurt you to protect whatever secrets that speech holds. Even if you don't run into one of them, it doesn't sound like it's going to be easy to get the speech out of the safe. I don't know about you, but I don't have a lot of experience with cracking safes."

I smiled ruefully. "Yeah, my experience with cracking safes open is about zero."

"So, what do you think?" Molly asked. "Should we wait until the morning, or should we go talk to Mitch tonight?"

"We might as well go talk to him tonight. It's hard to talk in the morning with everything I have to do to open the pie shop. Besides, it's probably better to just get it over with. But before we call Mitch, there is one more thing here I want to check."

"What's that?"

"I want to just pop into the men's restroom and make sure there aren't any windows in there that might have good vantage points to the field."

Molly made a face. "Do you really think someone like Tabitha would use the men's restroom?"

"Ordinarily, I would say no. She'd probably be even more disgusted by a dirty men's restroom than I would be. But if someone was trying to commit murder, they might be willing to do things they usually wouldn't."

"I guess you're right," Molly said reluctantly. "Let's go look. But let's make it quick. I don't want to get caught in the men's restroom."

I laughed. "What does it matter if someone sees you in there? Besides, no one's out here right now. This park isn't used much except for events, and there's obviously no event going on right now. No one's going to come by."

"Famous last words," Molly grumbled. "You probably just jinxed us."

I ignored her protests and made my way out of the women's restroom and into the men's restroom. The men's restroom was set up almost exactly like the women's restroom, with the addition of urinals instead of just stalls. It also had only one window, and that window was also blocked by a giant tree trunk.

I sighed. "Well, one thing I can say with absolute certainty is that if Tabitha did shoot Edgar, she didn't do it from either of these bathrooms."

"Good job, Sherlock," Molly said grumpily. "Now can we please get out of here?"

I nodded and started walking toward the door. But before I could get to it, it flew open. Molly yelped in surprise and I jumped backwards, a bit startled. Sprinkles let out a loud bark, and the man coming into the restroom also jumped a bit. But then, he saw it was us and started laughing.

"Theo!" I said. "What are you doing here? Are you following us?"

Theo laughed. "I could ask you the same thing. What are *you* doing? I'm just out for a run and needed to stop to take a leak. I wasn't expecting anyone to be in the restroom, especially not you two lovely ladies."

He arched a questioning eyebrow toward me, and I sighed. I could try to make up a story about what we were doing, but I couldn't imagine what I could say that wouldn't sound ridiculous. It wasn't exactly normal for two women to be hanging out in an empty public men's restroom at the same park where a murder had recently happened. Besides, Theo wasn't dumb. He probably had a rough idea of what we were doing out here. I decided to just be honest.

"We were trying to see whether either of these bathrooms provided a good vantage point for shooting Edgar out in the fields, because we're pretty sure Tabitha was in the bathroom when the shooting happened. But it looks like there's no way anyone could've shot him from inside either of these bathrooms. I'm not so sure that she was the one who killed Edgar after all."

"And have you shared these insights with Mitch?" Theo asked, even though I'm sure he already knew the answer.

"I was planning to," I said defensively. "But I hadn't had time to even leave the bathroom before you came barging in here."

Theo laughed. "Why are you acting like I'm the one who did something wrong? It's perfectly reasonable for me to be in here. You're the one in the wrong restroom."

He had a point, but I chose to ignore it. Sometimes he could be so maddeningly logical. Suddenly, that gave me an idea. His logic abilities might help me. Maybe if I told him everything I'd learned in the last twenty-four hours, he might have some insights on the case. If nothing else, he knew almost everyone in town, and he might know if anyone had secrets they were trying to hide. I knew that he'd want to tell Mitch about the speech in the safe as soon as he found out, but that was okay.

I was at the point where I needed to talk to Mitch, and I knew it. I might as well talk to Theo first and see if he had anything to add. This would delay talking to Mitch until tomorrow, but it would be worth it to have the chance to speak to Theo first.

"What are you doing this evening?" I asked.

Theo looked surprised by the question, but then grinned. "No plans, why? Are you asking me out on a date?"

I rolled my eyes at him. "No. But I do have some things about Edgar's murder that I'd like to discuss with you. Are you available for a chat with Molly and me?"

Theo considered this for a moment. "Sure, but you have to promise me you'll talk to Mitch after that. You know you need to, and he's going to kill me if he knows you're talking to me and not him."

"Deal. I think you're going to be very interested in what I found out."

Theo couldn't hide his eagerness. "Why don't the two of you come down to the Sunshine Springs Winery? I'll grab us a couple of bottles of wine and some food. The tasting room closes soon, but luckily I know the owner."

He winked at me, but I just shook my head at him. "You are the owner, you dork," I said in an exasperated tone.

Molly was raising an eyebrow at me, but I would explain to her on the drive over why I wanted to talk to Theo first. She'd understand.

And maybe, with Theo's perspective on everything I'd learned, we'd be one step closer to finding Edgar's murderer.

Chapter Nineteen

About fifteen minutes later, Molly, Theo and I arrived at the Sunshine Springs Winery's tasting room. Sprinkles had to wait outside again, but he didn't even complain about it this time. He was used to being left outside at the tasting room, and he knew by now that he would get a lot of attention here. Even after the tasting room closed, and the tourists all headed back into town for the night, there were still winery employees going in and out. They all knew Sprinkles by now, and they all loved him. He would be getting a lot of attention over the next hour or so while Molly, Theo and I were inside.

The last tourists were leaving just as we arrived, which was perfect. Theo himself went to the back kitchen and whipped us up a big plate of cheese, crackers and olives. The tasting room usually served small bites of these along with their wine tastings, but Theo made us a plate of them that was big enough to be considered dinner. He also grabbed us a few bottles of his favorite reserve Pinots.

As soon as we had settled down to eat, I dove right in and told Theo everything that had happened since I left Tabitha's house the night before. He wasn't happy that I'd ignored his advice about going home to rest, but he wasn't surprised. He only mildly reprimanded me for breaking my promise, because he was too interested in what I had learned to be truly mad at me.

When I'd finished telling him all about Edgar's safe and everything that Belinda had said, he sat in thoughtful silence for a few minutes. Finally, he gave Molly and me a big shrug.

"I don't know exactly what to think," he said. "This gives us the motive, for sure. I had thought it was weird that anyone would kill off Edgar for his inheritance when he was so old and about to die already, but this makes more sense. Someone wanted to make sure that he died before he told their secret."

"Exactly," I said. "But who?"

"I think we need to get a copy of that speech," Molly said. "We can sit around here and talk about it all night, but until we know exactly what's in that speech, we're just making uninformed guesses."

I knew she was right. But part of me had been hoping that once I told Theo everything, he would magically know who had a secret so big they were willing to kill for it. Unfortunately, he didn't seem to have any more ideas than I did. I decided to press him on Belinda, just to be sure.

"You've known Belinda Simmons for a long time, haven't you? Do you think it's possible that she would have killed Edgar to keep him quiet about her affair?"

Theo took a sip of wine and shook his head slowly. "I knew Belinda fairly well from the Morning Brew Café. Before your pie shop came along, that's where I always went if I wanted coffee while I was in town. I drank a lot of coffee over the years, and had a lot of interactions with Belinda. She always seemed friendly and kind. I guess you can't know someone all that well from interacting with them for a few minutes at a coffee shop, but she just doesn't strike me as the type of person who would kill someone. Tabitha seems a more likely suspect to me."

It was my turn to shake my head. "I don't think Tabitha is our killer. She's too much of a bumbling mess to organize shooting someone, and I'm almost positive she was in the bathroom the whole time the fireworks show was going on. She couldn't have shot him from inside there."

"You're *almost* positive," Theo said. "Key word being almost."

"Well," Molly said. "If it wasn't Belinda and it wasn't Tabitha, then we definitely need to get that speech. We have to figure out who the other suspects might be."

"True," I said. "Unless anyone thinks it's possible that it was Peter who shot his dad."

Theo looked over at me in surprise, and I realized that I hadn't mentioned anything about Peter in all of this.

"Peter? Why would you think Peter would shoot his own father? I know they didn't get along well, but that seems like a bit of a stretch."

"It is a bit of a stretch," I admitted. "But Peter was quite determined to keep his father from reading that speech. Do you think it's possible that he had a secret he was trying to hide that his father was planning to tell?"

"That's a good question," Theo said. "Ordinarily, I would have said no. Peter has always been a bit of a jerk, but part of his jerkiness has been his willingness to say whatever the hell he wants. He's always been one of those 'This is who I am and if you don't like it that's your problem' kind of guys. It would had to have been a pretty big, pretty nasty secret for him to kill over it, especially when the person he'd have to kill was his own father."

There was still some hesitation in Theo's voice.

"But?" I prompted.

"But...he's been acting strange lately."

Molly perked up with interest. "How so?"

"He's been hanging out at the winery a lot more than usual. He's always been a fairly regular customer at the tasting room, which is actually pretty rare among locals. Most locals get their wine in town and avoid the tourist crowds here at the tasting room. But I think Peter liked seeing fresh faces, and he showed up here often. Since his father's death, though, he's been here almost every evening—and he's been drinking more than just small tastings. I've seen him down a whole bottle of wine in one night. I think he's heartbroken."

"Well, of course he is," Molly said. "His dad just died. Even if he didn't get along with the guy, it was still his father. That has to bring up some feelings."

"Of course," Theo agreed. "But if you ask me, this has been more than just a little bit of grief over his dad dying. I would never have expected someone as stoic as Peter to act this way, especially when, let's be honest, his father and he were never all that close. I think it's possible that he's feeling some guilt."

"Guilt over killing his father?" I asked, stating the obvious.

Theo shrugged. "I don't know. I'm just saying it's a possibility. Mitch will have to get a copy of that speech and see if there are any secrets about Peter in there. If there are, then I think you have your answer."

I was both excited and disappointed by this news. If Peter was feeling guilty over his father's death, then perhaps we had finally found the murderer. But without something more to go on, it was quite a jump to say that Peter acting guilty meant that he had killed his father.

It looked like I had really, truly reached the end of the line. I couldn't delay things another day. I had to bring Mitch into this. Someone had to look at a copy of that speech, although I knew I wouldn't be the one looking at it. Mitch didn't like me sticking my nose in his investigations, and I couldn't think of any way I could possibly convince him that I deserved to see that speech.

I felt a little bit angry at that thought. I wished there was some way I could be involved in the grand finale of this case, but it didn't look like that was in the cards for me. I took another sip of my wine, contemplating the unfairness of life, when suddenly I heard Sprinkles starting to bark up a storm. Theo, Molly and I all glanced toward the tasting room's door.

"What's wrong with Sprinkles?" Molly asked.

I hopped off my barstool and started toward the door. "I don't know, but that's not a happy bark."

I felt my stomach twisting up in a worried knot. This frantic bark was nothing like Sprinkles' normal, laidback yips. But before I could reach the door, it flew open. One of the winery employees came rushing in, and Sprinkles bounded in after him, still barking like crazy.

"Boss!" the man said to Theo. "You better come quick! There's a man in the vineyard who's drunk out of his mind. He's crashing around and ruining the grapes, but I can't get him to leave."

Theo was on his feet in an instant, running toward the door. "Any idea who it is? One of the tourists, maybe?"

"No, I don't think it's a tourist," the employee said. "Looks like that local guy who's always coming in and drinking a bottle a night. I think he had more than just one bottle tonight, though."

"Peter?" Theo asked.

The employee nodded vigorously. "Yeah, that's the one. Peter."

Theo went racing out the door toward the vineyard without another word. Sprinkles, Molly and I ran hot on his heels.

Chapter Twenty

The summer sun had just disappeared over the horizon, casting a hazy, orange glow over the grapevines. I loved this time of day, when the world was slowing down and preparing to sleep. I'd been out at the grapevines in twilight a few times, and I loved the way the grapes seemed to glow in the orange sunset. Soon, those same grapes would be glowing from the shimmering moonlight. Since moving to Sunshine Springs, I'd learned that few places in the world were more peaceful than a vineyard at night.

But tonight, Theo's vineyard was anything but peaceful. It didn't take long to figure out where the drunken man was. He sounded like an elephant as he crashed through a row of prizewinning Pinot grapes. The moment I caught a glimpse of him, I knew it was definitely Peter.

A few of Theo's employees who hadn't yet gone home for the day were trying to corral him, but he swung his fists anytime they got near. I couldn't help but feel amazed at how much punch Peter packed for a nearly seventy-year-old man. He yelled a string of expletives at them, slurring his words horribly but getting his point across.

Sprinkles bounded ahead of us, barking wildly to sound the alarm—just in case anyone hadn't yet noticed the angry man careening around ahead of us. I slowed to a fast walk as we got closer, then stopped altogether a safe distance away. There were several strong men around. No need to jump into the fray myself. I didn't think my unimpressive muscles were going to do anything to bring Peter under control.

Theo didn't hold back, though. As he approached Peter, I marveled at how calm he was acting. If those had been my grapevines getting trampled, I would have probably been punching Peter's daylights out, no matter how unimpressive my muscles.

But Theo walked up to Peter slowly, speaking in a soothing voice as he did.

"Peter, it's me. Theo. You know me, right? The guy who owns this winery."

Peter stopped swinging his fists around for a moment and tried to focus his bloodshot eyes on Theo.

"Oh, I know you alright. You're the only perfect one in this town, it seems."

Molly looked over at me and arched her eyebrow. "What does he mean by that?" she whispered.

"Beats me," I whispered back. Sprinkles whined beside me, but I quietly shushed him. I wanted to hear what else Peter had to say.

"My dad couldn't stand any of the business owners in this town," Peter continued in his slurry voice. "He hated all of them, and thought they were all crooked. Even me! He didn't support his own son! But you, Theo…you he loved. He sang your praises all the time. He'd go on and on and on about how wonderful you were. I don't know what you did to impress him so much, but he couldn't say a single bad thing about you. Must be nice to be admired so much."

Peter swung a fist in Theo's direction, but he was too far away to have any hope of actually hitting Theo. Not only that, but Peter was so drunk that the momentum from swinging his fist sent him totally off balance. He fell over onto his side onto a grapevine, grunting in pain as he landed.

"Ow! These things are more dangerous than they look," he said as he tried unsuccessfully to disentangle himself from the vines.

Theo let out a long sigh, then looked over at his employees. "You boys can go home. I can take it from here."

"Are you sure, boss?" one of the men asked. He looked doubtfully over at Peter, who was still thrashing around, ruining the vine.

"I'm sure," Theo said. "I know this guy. I'm sure I'll be able to handle him, and I don't want you all to have to stay past your work hours. It's been a long day. Go home and relax."

Theo's employees still looked unsure, but when he made a shooing motion at them with his hands, they shrugged and started heading off. Peter let out a long, drunken laugh as they walked off.

"Called off your dogs, did you?" he asked Theo. "Wouldn't want them to beat me up and ruin your reputation as the perfect man, now would you?"

"I don't know what you're talking about," Theo answered. "I'm not perfect. I do my best to run this winery in a way that would make my father proud, may he rest in peace. But I'm not perfect. No one is, no matter what your own father told you. Now, come on. Why don't you come to the tasting room with us and have something to eat? It'll help stave off the nasty headache you've got coming."

I was sure that Peter was going to protest. He was acting so wildly belligerent that I was sure there was no way he'd simply give up and agree to head back to the tasting room with us. But to my surprise, Peter looked at Theo with squinty eyes, and then burst into tears.

"Okay. I'll come back. It's been a long time since I've had dinner with friends at the tasting room."

I looked at Molly and rolled my eyes. "Drunk people," I said.

She shrugged. "Pretty much. But at least he's going to come willingly."

Theo wasted no time in helping Peter stand up. I knew he probably wanted to get back to the tasting room and away from the vineyards before Peter changed his mind and started crashing around in the grapevines again. As we walked back, Peter alternated between sobbing and laughing hysterically.

Normally, I would have made myself scarce as quickly as possible in a situation like this. I wouldn't have wanted to hang around to help babysit a drunken man who was showing a penchant for acting violent. But this was different. This drunken man was a possible suspect, and I was eager to see whether he might say something that would incriminate himself in his father's murder.

When we got to the tasting room and went inside, Peter made a beeline for the counter, where our food was still sitting. But when he saw the crackers, olives, and cheese, he made a face.

"This is all you have? I was hoping for something a little different. I'm so tired of these olives and crackers. I've been eating them for dinner every night since my father died."

"That's the only food we serve at the winery," Theo said. He kept his voice soothing, but I could hear the underlying note of frustration. No doubt, every moment that passed made it harder for him not to fly off the handle at Peter.

"I want something else," Peter whined, sounding like an unreasonable toddler.

"I'm sorry. We don't have anything else. I could order a pizza to be delivered here, if you'd like. But that will take about half an hour."

"I hate pizza!" Peter said, slamming his fist on the counter top. I could see he was about to devolve back into an angry, drunken rage, and I quickly stepped in.

"What about pie?" I asked. "I have a key lime pie in my car that's left over from today's sales at the café."

Peter turned to look at me, as though noticing me for the first time. "Hey, you're the pie lady."

I gulped. Was he going to get angry again at just the sight of me? Our last encounter hadn't exactly ended with us being best buddies. I tried not to let my fear show, and smiled brightly at him instead. "Yup, I'm the pie lady. Do you like key lime?"

Theo gave me a look that said I was crazy. "Izzy! Your pies have alcohol in them! Do you really think that's the best thing to feed to a man who's already drunk out of his mind?"

"There's not that much alcohol in my pies!" I protested. "It gets baked out. Besides, this one isn't an alcoholic pie. It's one I was saving for Sprinkles, but I'm sure he's happy to share, given the circumstances."

Beside me, Sprinkles whined disapprovingly. He was never happy to share his pie, no matter how much I claimed he was. I looked down at him in surprise. I hadn't realized that he'd followed us into the tasting room.

"Sprinkles! You know you're not allowed in here! You're supposed to wait outside!"

Theo shook his head wearily. "It's alright. It's after hours, and he's not going to bother any of us. My guess is that he wants to stick close to you to protect you."

Theo glanced over at Peter as he said this, and I knew he was right. Sprinkles didn't trust Peter to behave. Neither did any of us, really, but we were tolerating Peter because we wanted to know what he might be able to tell us about his father's murder.

"I love key lime," Peter exclaimed while we were all staring warily at him. "Where's my pie?"

"I'll run out to my car and get it right now," I said. Then I turned to Sprinkles. "Alright, buddy. You can stay inside. But at least come with me to get the pie."

Sprinkles wagged his spotted tail triumphantly, then went with me to get the pie. Five minutes later, I had placed a slice of pie in front of everyone, even Sprinkles. Sprinkles chowed down on the pie with gusto, and Theo watched with a fascinated but disapproving look on his face.

"That dog of yours is going to get cavities," he said. "And possibly diabetes."

"No he's not. I brush his teeth every night. And I limit the amount of pie I feed him. At least, I try to. It's hard when he looks up at you with those soulful brown eyes."

"This pie is worth cavities," Molly said as she shoved a big bite of it into her mouth.

Theo and I didn't touch our slices. We were too busy waiting for Peter to talk. Peter sat on a barstool, swaying back and forth in a stupor while he ate his pie. I kept expecting him to fall over, but he somehow managed to stay upright. He seemed to be calming down as he ate, and when he finished the first slice of pie, I hurriedly placed a second slice in front of him. I wanted him to keep eating and sobering up so that he didn't behave so violently, but I didn't want him to sober up too much. At least not until he'd talked a bit and spilled all his secrets.

Would he say something helpful to us? I wished Theo would try to prod him a little bit with questions, but Theo didn't seem interested in poking the bear. I couldn't blame him for that, since Peter had already done significant damage to one of Theo's grapevines. Theo was probably worrying about what other damage Peter might do if he turned into an angry drunk again. But as Peter finished his second slice of pie, I couldn't be patient any longer. I didn't want to lose a chance to talk to Peter while his defenses were down.

"Why do you think your dad didn't support you?" I asked. "You're such a successful businessman. Surely, he must have been at least a little bit proud of you."

I ignored the warning look Theo gave me and concentrated all of my attention on Peter. As I'd expected, Peter's eyes darkened at my question. But thankfully, he didn't go into an all-out rage again. He did slam his fists on the counter top a few times, but we were all fine with that. As long as he kept punching the counter and not us, I wasn't going to complain.

"My dad wasn't the least bit proud of me," Peter said bitterly. "He thought I was a hack, and that my business wasn't legitimate. Marketing wasn't a respectable career, in his opinion. Never mind the fact that marketing made me rich. It still wasn't a real job."

"Sounds rough," I said mildly. He seemed to be on a roll, and I didn't want to say too much and interrupt his momentum.

"It was very rough," Peter continued, gathering enthusiasm for his rant as he spoke. "My father never loved me. Even as I got older myself, and proved that I'd been smart enough to build a strong business, he couldn't be proud of me. I'm sixty-seven years old, and my father still treated me like I was only an irresponsible child."

To my right, I saw Theo and Molly watching Peter, hanging on to every word. We all wanted him to say something to incriminate himself, but so far every word had been merely a complaint about Edgar. Complaining about Edgar wasn't enough on its own to prove that Peter had killed Edgar. We needed something more.

Or perhaps Peter was another dead end. Perhaps he was innocent, just like I'd come to believe Tabitha was. Theo seemed to think that Belinda was innocent as well. My three top suspects were turning out to be not as murderous as I'd thought, but I told myself that my investigations hadn't been a total loss. Even if I hadn't discovered the murderer, I'd learned about the speech. That was a huge step forward. I still believed that as soon as a copy of that speech was found, things were going to become a lot clearer.

But I wasn't ready to give up on Peter completely. Perhaps he just needed a bit of prodding.

"Maybe your father was proud of you, and just didn't know how to show it. Some people are like that, you know."

Theo glared at me, but I ignored him once again. My comment had its desired effect, and Peter started becoming even angrier. I crossed my fingers that this anger would result in Peter talking more, and not in Peter causing more damage to Theo's winery.

I was in luck. Peter pounded the counter once more, then continued his ranting.

"My father knew how to show people he was proud of them. Look at Frank Simmons. My father sang that man's praises night and day to anyone who would listen. He thought that Frank was the best handyman to ever walk the face of the earth, and he recommended his work to all his friends. And then, there was Theo here."

Peter turned and spat in Theo's direction, but luckily Theo was far enough away that the spit didn't hit him. I saw anger flare in Theo's eyes, but Theo didn't act on that anger. He waited quietly to see what else Peter might say.

"My father thought Theo was the town's best businessman. And this winery is run well, I'll give you that. But what about my business? It brings in a ton of revenue. I started it from scratch, with nothing but my own hard work and brains. But my father still considers me a failure."

"I'm sure he at least appreciates your brains," Molly piped in. "If I remember right, you went to Harvard, didn't you? When you opened your business, everyone in Sunshine Springs kept talking about how lucky we were to have a Harvard businessman right here in our little town."

I was sure Molly intended her comment as a compliment, but when she finished speaking, Peter exploded with more anger than he'd shown since we'd come into the tasting room.

"What does it matter where I went to school? Nothing I ever did would have made my father proud. He was determined to hate me! I don't even know why I care, anyway. I should just let it go. He was a crazy old man who wanted to spend his last days harassing people because they weren't perfect. He couldn't just be nice, could he? It was bad enough he didn't leave me any inheritance. He also couldn't say one nice thing about me in the speech he wanted to give at his hundredth birthday party, could he? Oh, no. He was determined to ruin my life and everyone else's!"

Peter's face had turned purple with rage. He banged his fist on the counter a few more times, and then, all of a sudden, he slumped over. His face landed smack in the middle of what remained of his key lime pie. For a few shocked moments, Molly, Theo and I just stared at him.

"What just happened?" I asked hesitantly. "Is he still breathing? Did he have a heart attack or something?"

Theo started walking toward him. "My guess is that he's passed out from being so drunk, but I guess we should make sure."

Theo gave Peter a little nudge, but Peter didn't move. Theo nudged harder, and Peter's head rolled sideways. His face was covered with pie, just like a clown who'd been pied in the face at the circus. I held my breath as Theo went to check his pulse. Had one of our suspects just died on us?

But before Theo could find a pulse, Peter coughed, sending little pieces of pie flying from his face across the counter. A moment later, he started snoring loudly.

"I don't think he's dead," Molly observed.

Sprinkles whined and flopped down to lie on the floor in disgust. I had a feeling he was protesting the fact that I'd wasted a perfectly good slice of pie by giving it to a drunken man who was only going to nosedive into it. But I was glad I'd sacrificed the pie. Peter had said what I needed to know. I stood there in silence, thinking over everything Peter had just said, and processing it until I was sure.

Everything suddenly made sense. I turned to Molly in excitement. "Get your keys! We need to get going!"

"What? To where?"

"To Edgar Bates' house. We'll call Mitch on the way and tell him to meet us there."

Molly was already digging in her purse for her keys. "Did you figure out something else that might have been in Edgar's speech?"

I nodded, my excitement mounting. "I think I have a pretty good idea of what was in that speech, and I know who the killer was."

"You do?" Theo piped in. "Who? And how did you figure it out?"

"Something Peter said tipped me off. And you'll see who soon enough." I wasn't about to tell him now so that he could be the one to tell Mitch first. I wanted to get the credit for figuring this out.

I motioned to Molly and Sprinkles, and started running toward the door.

"Wait a minute!" Theo said. "You're just going to leave me here alone with this snoring drunk while you take off to find the speech?"

I paused for a moment to look back at Theo. "Yup. Sorry. No time to wait. I'm sure Peter will be in a better mood when he wakes up, anyway. Although you might want to have some ibuprofen on hand. He's probably going to have a killer headache."

I turned to leave again, ignoring Theo's protests. I didn't have time to sit around and wait for a snoring drunk to wake up.

Not when I had just solved a murder case. All of my sleuthing efforts had finally paid off.

Chapter Twenty-One

I let Molly drive, and as she sped down the road toward Edgar Bates' house, I dialed Mitch on my cell phone.

"Izzy," he said in greeting, not even bothering to say hello first. Thanks to caller I.D., he knew it was me. He also knew that if I was calling him at this hour, it probably had something to do with a case he was working on. He didn't even try to hide the annoyance in his voice, and I was sure he was preparing a lecture for me on why I should leave the detective work to him.

I didn't give him a chance to launch into that lecture.

"Listen, I know you're going to be mad at me, but save the lectures for later. I have a lot to tell you."

I launched into a complete explanation of everything that I had learned about Edgar's murder. Some of it Mitch already knew, but the bit about the safe and the speech surprised him. He knew that Edgar had a safe, but he hadn't been in too much of a rush to look inside. He'd just assumed that it was full of more valuables that would need to be sold along with the rest of Edgar's assets.

"Now that you mention it," Mitch said. "I do remember Peter being a little weird about the speech. I guess I never thought much of it. I assumed that there was nothing more to it than Peter being embarrassed of his dad's ramblings."

"That's what Peter wanted you to believe. But in reality, Peter knew that that speech contained secrets that would cause a lot of trouble for a lot of people in Sunshine Springs. And something he said at the winery tonight tipped me off about which secret Peter thought was most worrisome, and who the murderer was."

"Who?" Mitch demanded.

"Meet me at Edgar's house and I'll tell you," I said. Then I hung up the phone before Mitch could protest. I'm sure I was driving him crazy. But if I gave away all my information, then he would just order me not to show up at the house and to leave everything to him. I needed him to need me at least a little bit, so that I could still be involved with all of this.

When I hung up the phone, Molly immediately demanded to know what I knew.

"Enough with the theatrics, Izzy," she said. "You can put off Theo and Mitch, but don't leave me hanging. I'm your best friend. Tell me what you know! What did you figure out? Who killed Edgar?"

I had every intention of telling Molly. Truly, I did. But by then we were pulling into Edgar's driveway, and I was distracted by the fact that there was a large moving van in that driveway.

"Yikes," I said. "Something tells me that whoever is responsible for that moving van isn't here on official business."

"You're right," Molly said. "Look over there."

I looked in the direction that Molly's finger was pointing, and I wasn't surprised to see Tabitha coming out of Edgar's front door. She was wearing one of her ridiculously tight dresses, but at least she'd chosen footwear other than high heels today. She had on a pair of tennis shoes—sparkly, hot pink tennis shoes, but tennis shoes nonetheless. She was pushing a furniture dolly out the front door with some difficulty, and my eyes nearly bugged out of my head when I saw what was on that dolly.

"Is that Edgar's safe?" I asked, almost not believing what I was seeing.

Molly squinted over at the furniture dolly. "I think it is. Looks like Tabitha is about to run away with the speech."

"Oh no she's not!" I jumped out of the car before it had even come to a complete stop, and started running towards Tabitha.

"Hey! What do you think you're doing?" I shouted.

Tabitha looked up and her eyes filled with panic when she saw me.

"Get away from me," she screamed. "You're nothing but trouble, and you have no right to be here!"

"You have no right to be here either," I yelled. "And you especially have no right to take that safe."

"I'll take whatever I want, and you can't stop me!"

"We'll see about that," I said as I lunged for the safe. Tabitha screamed at me in a voice that sounded like a howling monkey, and then tackled me with surprising strength. I didn't know what sort of aerobics videos she normally did, but they must have focused heavily on arm exercises. She wrestled me to the ground with surprising ease.

But I wasn't giving up easily. I'd done a few Tae Bo workouts in my day, too. I let out a roar that was intended to be intimidating, but probably sounded more desperate than anything. Still, it was a solid effort.

I pushed Tabitha off of me and lunged for the safe again. In response, she howled and made another attempt to tackle me. I could tell that I was going to have quite a few bruises and sore muscles tomorrow, but it didn't matter. All that mattered in that moment was making sure that Tabitha didn't make off with the safe.

Molly finished parking the car, and she and Sprinkles came running over. Molly was yelling at us to stop, and Sprinkles was running around us in circles, barking nonstop. He probably would have attacked Tabitha if it hadn't been for the fact that Mitch and several other police officers drove up at that moment.

When Tabitha saw the three police cruisers coming in with their lights flashing, she abandoned her fight with me. She stood and took off running toward the moving van, leaving the safe and the furniture dolly behind. Then she fired up the engine, and didn't let the fact that Molly's car was blocking the driveway slow her down.

Tabitha started driving over the grass of Edgar's expansive front lawn, trying to make her way to the road. But Mitch's police officers saw what was happening and quickly drove up to block the spot where Tabitha was trying to drive over the curb and onto the street.

Tabitha still wasn't giving up. She threw the truck into reverse and tried to adjust her course so that she could leave from another spot on the curb, but the police cruisers just followed her. Finally, she seemed to realize that it was hopeless. She killed the engine on the truck, jumped out, and started running across the lawn in a desperate attempt to escape on foot. As I sat up slowly, brushing the dirt and grass from my shirt and pants, I saw Mitch shake his head in exasperation. He looked over at one of his officers.

"Go catch her and put some handcuffs on her," he said. "I'm tired of chasing her around."

It only took a few moments for the officers to catch Tabitha. In her haste, she tripped and fell face first into the grass, sending one of her sparkling pink shoes flying right off her foot. As the officers moved to cuff her, she started screaming at them. She yelled that they had no right to arrest her, and that she was only taking what rightfully belonged to her. Mitch huffed in annoyance, and then turned his attention back to me.

"What in the world were you doing wrestling with Tabitha?"

"Protecting evidence, of course! She was trying to make off with the safe."

Mitch cracked his knuckles, and I flinched in annoyance at the sound. But I didn't dare complain about it right now. Mitch let out a long sigh, and then reached down to offer me a hand up. Once I was standing, he looked over me with a scrutinizing eye.

"Are you all right?"

"I'm fine. I'm sure I look like a hot mess, but I'm fine."

Sprinkles came running up to me, nudging one of my hands and giving it several licks. Then he sat down beside me protectively, the look in his eyes daring anyone else to try to attack me. Molly was standing nearby too, looking stunned.

"I can't believe Tabitha tackled you like that," she said.

Mitch scowled at both of us. "Oh, come on. Don't act so surprised. She pulled a gun on you last time you were here. And from what you told me on the phone a few minutes ago, this safe has a speech inside of it that will provide evidence about who murdered Edgar Bates. Let me guess: Tabitha murdered him, and she was trying to make off with the safe so that there wouldn't be evidence against her."

I shook my head. "She was making off with the safe because she thinks there are expensive valuables in there. But I don't think she has a clue that there was actually a speech in there, or that it was important. Tabitha isn't the murderer."

Mitch looked genuinely shocked by this. "She isn't? Then who is?"

"Is it Belinda?" Molly asked.

Before I could say anything else, Tabitha was suddenly screaming again, and struggling to break free from the officers despite the fact that she was handcuffed.

"What is *he* doing here?" she yelled. "If I don't have the right to be here, then neither does he!"

I turned to see Theo driving up in his black Mercedes. But it wasn't Theo that Tabitha was upset about. In the passenger seat, still completely passed out, sat Peter. He was buckled in, but had fallen over so that his unconscious face was smashed against the glass of the window. It was quite an unflattering look, but it was clear that it was Peter.

"What in the world?" Mitch said, echoing what we all must have been thinking.

Theo climbed out of the car and glared at me. "I can't believe you left me at the winery with that drunken fool."

"I needed to get here right away," I said. "And it's a good thing I didn't wait for you or Peter, because if I hadn't gotten here when I did, Tabitha might have made off with the safe. Why did you drag Peter out here, anyway?"

"Because I wasn't about to miss this! And if being here to see how this all went down meant risking a drunken guy possibly vomiting all over my Mercedes' leather seats, then so be it. I would have sent you the bill for the cleaning."

"And I wouldn't have paid it!" I retorted. "It's not my fault that you didn't just leave Peter behind at the winery. He would have slept it off eventually."

"I couldn't just leave him there! What if he woke up and started thrashing around in my grapevines again? He's already ruined enough of them. Or what if he woke up still drunk and decided to try to drive off? He could have killed himself or someone else. I had no choice but to take him with me so that he didn't cause any trouble."

I opened my mouth to make another retort, but Mitch interrupted our little spat.

"Enough! There's no need for either of you to be here, and I have a good mind to order you both to leave right now."

"You can't make me leave," Theo said. "I'm on the street, not on Edgar's property. The street is public property and I have every right to be here."

Mitch cracked his knuckles. "Not if you're interfering with my attempts to get evidence on a murder."

Molly and I glanced at each other in surprise. I didn't think I'd ever seen Mitch and Theo fighting before, which meant Mitch must have reached the absolute end of his patience. I thought things couldn't possibly get any crazier, but then they did.

I saw another expensive black Mercedes pulling up, and I recognized the man inside as Edgar's lawyer. Tabitha recognized him too, and she wasn't happy to see him.

"What is he doing here? He's the one who cheated me out of my portion of Edgar's estate!"

No one bothered to correct her. I was sure the lawyer had already explained to her about a thousand times that he himself wasn't the one who had actually written the will. Edgar had done that, and had clearly not wanted Tabitha to get anything.

I can't imagine why, I thought sarcastically. How had Edgar managed to live with Tabitha for more than a day without going crazy?

"I called Edgar's lawyer out here because he's the only one who has the combination to the safe," Mitch said. "Rather than trying to drill the safe open to get the speech out, I thought we might as well do things the easy way."

"Indeed," Edgar's lawyer said as he approached the safe. "But how in the world did you get the safe out here? It was secured to an inside wall with heavy duty steel rods. It wasn't exactly something you could just pick up and move."

"I didn't move it out here," Mitch said. "Tabitha did. She was trying to make off with it when I arrived."

"Luckily," I interrupted, "*I* arrived in time to stop Tabitha from actually making off with it."

I glared at Mitch. I wasn't going to let him forget that I had played a part in making sure the safe didn't disappear before he arrived. Mitch glared right back at me.

Edgar's lawyer shook his head and whistled. "Well, Tabitha must be pretty good with power tools. She would have needed some serious power to disconnect the safe from the wall."

The image of Tabitha in her tight dress and sparkling sneakers wielding a power tool struck me as funny, and I couldn't help but laugh. Mitch, however, was not amused.

"Well, however Tabitha did it, this safe is out here now. Let's open it so I can review this speech that Izzy seems to think will reveal who the murderer is."

"Right away," Edgar's lawyer said, and stepped up to enter the combination. Within moments, the safe was opened and we were all peering inside. Mitch tried to push us back, but we ignored him and looked over his shoulder.

The safe had quite a hodgepodge of items. I saw jewelry, some items that looked like small antiques, and mountains of papers. On the very top of the papers a manila envelope rested. Mitch pulled out the envelope, opened it, and scanned the contents for a few seconds. Then he nodded.

"This is it," he said, his eyes shining. "This is Edgar's speech."

"What does it say?" I demanded, stepping over to try to look at it.

Mitch stepped back. "No way. I need to review this first. It's official evidence, and not for public consumption."

I had expected this, but I made a face at him nonetheless. Mitch barely noticed. His eyes started moving across the paper as he silently read the speech. We all stared at him and held our breath. A few moments later, his eyes widened.

"No way," he said in a voice that was barely more than a whisper. "That can't be true!"

Just then, we heard the sound of pounding coming from Theo's car. We all turned our attention to the black Mercedes, where an angry-looking Peter was now awake, opening the door, and stumbling out.

Things were about to get interesting.

Chapter Twenty-Two

"Where am I?" Peter asked.

He looked around in confusion for a few moments, until understanding dawned on his face.

"I'm at my dad's house," he said, more to himself than to anyone else. His eyes focused first on Theo, then on me, and finally on Mitch.

His confusion returned. He must have been wondering why we were all standing in the front yard.

"How did I get here? And why are you all here?"

"I brought you over," Theo said. "I needed to get here, and I couldn't leave you alone at the winery when you were passed out drunk."

"I'm not drunk," Peter said. But then he tried to take a step forward and stumbled. He might not be as drunk as he had been, but he still wasn't completely sober. A moment later, his eyes fell on Tabitha and his temper returned.

"Why is she still here? If I can't be here going through my dad's stuff, then neither can she. This is so unfair, but what did I really expect? The police here are a joke."

Peter looked back in Mitch's direction, and that's when he realized that his father's lawyer was also there, standing next to the open safe. I had never seen the color drain out of someone's face so quickly.

"Hey! What are you boys doing! That's my dad safe! It's private property!"

Peter started stumbling forward, and I quickly stepped out of his way as he approached the safe. I certainly wasn't going to be the one to fight him off. But when he looked in the safe, he must have immediately realized that the document he was looking for was gone. He whirled around and saw Mitch holding the speech.

Peter roared angrily and made a grab for the manila folder, but Mitch stepped out of the way. That wasn't that hard to do, since Peter currently had about all the coordination of a giant cow.

"That's not yours! Give it back!" Peter yelled.

Mitch nodded at one of his officers, who walked over to help restrain Peter. Peter swung around wildly, but the officer quickly subdued him by threatening handcuffs if he didn't cooperate.

"This isn't private property," Mitch said. "This safe and everything else in the house technically belongs to the city now. It's part of the assets that are to be liquidated and sold as your father instructed."

In response, Peter angrily lunged towards Mitch once again. One of the police officers grabbed him and held him back, but Mitch merely raised an eyebrow at him.

"I've just been reading this speech," Mitch said, waving the manila folder around. "There are quite a few interesting things in here. Is there anything you'd like to tell me?"

"The only thing I want to tell you is that I'm going to sue you for libel," Peter yelled. "I'll take you down in court for slander if you release any of the information about me in that speech!"

I cleared my throat. "Actually, Peter, you can't take Mitch down if whatever is said about you in that speech is true. According to the law, truth is an absolute defense against a slander or libel charge."

Theo laughed, and then sang out, "The more you know!"

Peter wasn't amused. He turned his angry eyes toward me. "And how would a pie shop owner know anything about the law?"

Molly stepped forward and jabbed her finger in my direction. "That pie shop owner worked as a lawyer for a big firm before opening her café, so I'd say she knows a thing or two about the law. Not only that, but she's also my best friend, so don't you dare insult her."

Peter glanced over at me in surprise. I didn't like to mention the fact that I was a lawyer, since I was trying to leave that part of my life behind. But on occasion, my legal knowledge did come in handy. This had been one of those occasions. Peter glared at me, and then looked over at his father's lawyer.

"I'm sure you can tell me that what Izzy's saying isn't correct."

Edgar's lawyer shrugged. "Actually, she's right. You can't sue someone for telling the truth about you."

"Which begs the question," Mitch interrupted, waving the speech around in the air. "*Is* this true?"

It took all the restraint I had not to reach over and grab the speech out of Mitch's hands. I was dying to know what it said.

Peter didn't respond for a moment, and Mitch waved the speech again for emphasis.

"Well?" Mitch prompted.

"Of course it's not true! None of it's true. That whole speech is ridiculous."

"The whole speech?" Mitch said. "I'd have to disagree with you there, because I know from personal experience that several of the things your dad said in here are, in fact, true. Which makes me wonder, why would he write what he did about you if it wasn't true?"

"Because he was trying to ruin me! Don't you get it? My dad couldn't stand that I was successful, and he wanted to bring me down."

Mitch shrugged. "I guess that's possible, although it seems strange for a father to want to ruin his own son like that. But it will be easy enough to find out the truth. All I have to do is make a few phone calls and verify whether your diploma is legitimate. Then I'll know whether your dad was crazy or not, won't I?"

His diploma, I wondered. What was Mitch talking about? I glanced at Molly and then at Theo. They looked as eager as I was to know what was in that speech, but it didn't look like Mitch was going to be very forthcoming with the contents.

That was all right, because in the next moment, Peter broke down completely.

"Alright, alright! It's true!" Peter dissolved for a few moments into drunken sobs, then he stumbled and completely fell over onto the grass. He sat there with his head in his hands, heaving out more great, drunken sobs. I had to strain to understand what he was saying, but if I listened hard enough, I could comprehend his words.

"I don't know why it mattered so much to my dad that I didn't actually go to Harvard. He thought it was wrong to lie about that, but I've proven over the last several decades that I was a good businessman. I just used my fake Harvard diploma to get my foot in the door. Once my foot was in, the rest of the business was all hard work. I was successful because of my smarts and hard work, not because of any diploma. I don't know why my dad couldn't just accept that and leave me be."

Molly and I looked at each other in confusion. When I glanced at Theo, he looked just as confused.

"Wait a minute," Theo said. "You're saying you didn't actually go to Harvard?"

"No, I didn't go to Harvard. So sue me." Peter looked sullenly up at Theo.

"But you always brag about your Harvard education," Theo said. "I've got to be honest, you've always been a bit of a jerk, and no one in town really liked you. But people gave you a chance and continued to do business with you because they thought you were so highly educated. Now you're telling me all of that was a lie?"

Peter didn't say anything in response to that.

"It was a lie, wasn't it?" Mitch asked. "Your dad might have been an ornery old man, but he was an honest old man. He couldn't stand it that you'd lied to the whole town about where you went to school just to get your business started. He kept quiet for a long time because he couldn't bring himself to tell a secret that he knew would ruin his own son's business. But you never fully appreciated him, did you? You were always fighting with him. And toward the end of his life, he must have decided he was done with keeping your secrets."

Peter still remained silent.

"Wow," I said. "I never would have guessed that you'd lied about going to Harvard. You're a pretty good liar, and that's not a compliment."

Mitch looked over at me. "I thought you said you knew who the killer was. Are you telling me it's not Peter?"

"Oh, it's Peter," I said.

Mitch looked confused. "But you just said that you never would have guessed that he'd lied about Harvard. I thought you said you knew what was in the speech, and you knew that it would show who the killer was."

I shrugged. "At the winery today I realized that there must be something in the speech that related to ruining Peter's business. I didn't know exactly what the secret was, but from the way Peter was talking it was clear that he thought his father intended to bring down his business. Peter wasn't happy that his cover was about to be blown, and he tried to convince his dad not to give the speech. But Edgar was determined. In his final days, he wanted to reveal the truth about everything—including the truth about his son's education. Peter might not have cared enough about his father's inheritance to kill him for that, but Peter does care about his business. It's his entire life. It's how he made his own fortune, and it's what gives him his sense of identity here in the community."

"He cared about it so much, that he was willing to kill his dad to make sure his secret never got out," Theo said, starting to piece the puzzle together.

I nodded. "Exactly."

"This all makes sense now," Mitch said slowly. "No one ever liked Peter, and no one would have given him a chance at opening up a business if it hadn't been for the fact that he went to Harvard. But he built his business on the strength of that alone. If people in Sunshine Springs knew they'd been lied to, they would stop patronizing his business altogether."

We all looked over at Peter, who sat sniffling in the grass. His hair stuck out every which way, and his usually crisp dress shirt was quite wrinkled at this point. I held my breath, waiting for his next excuse. But he seemed to have run out of excuses. His eyes turned dark with anger, and he pounded his fist on the grass. "He was trying to destroy my life! Can anyone blame me for taking his?"

My eyes widened. It sounded very much like Peter had just confessed that he was the one who had killed his dad. I had been pretty certain that he was the killer, but I had never expected him to break down and confess that easily. No one had. As I looked around, there were shocked looks on everyone's faces—even Tabitha's.

Mitch was the first to regain his composure. He stepped toward Peter and pulled a pair of handcuffs from his side belt. "Peter Bates, you're under arrest for the murder of Edgar Bates."

We all stared as Mitch told Peter his rights and fastened the handcuffs on him. As Mitch pulled Peter to his feet and started leading him toward one of the cop cars, I saw Molly pull her cell phone out of her pocket. She held it up and turned around to take a selfie of herself with Mitch, Peter, and the cop cars in the background.

"Really?" I asked. "You're taking a selfie of that?"

She grinned at me. "Why not? You know this is going be the top gossip in town. I might as well have proof that I was here for the grand event of Peter Bates' arrest. Besides, I'm starting to have quite a collection of selfies with myself and a murderer being arrested in the background. Wouldn't want to miss out on a chance to add to that collection."

I groaned. "I swear, you only help me with my detective work so that you get the chance to take a selfie when the case is solved."

Molly grinned and shrugged. "So? Regardless of the reason, I still helped you, didn't I?"

I smiled at her. "I suppose you did. I guess I at least owe you a slice of pie. I'll bake you whatever kind you want."

"Hey," Theo said. "I helped, too. Do I get pie?"

I thought about teasing Theo and telling him that he hadn't helped nearly as much as Molly, but I decided against it. I was just happy that this case was solved and that order had once again been restored to Sunshine Springs.

"Sure, why not? Pie for everyone! Why don't you to come over and join me at the café after closing time tomorrow? We can eat pie and drink wine, toasting the fact that another murder case has been solved."

"I'll toast to that," Theo said. "See you tomorrow."

He started off toward his car, and I started to walk toward Molly's car. But she grabbed my arm and stopped me.

"Wait just a minute. You know you want one, too." She held her phone up and took a selfie of me and her together with the police in the background. Sprinkles barked, and I laughed.

"Okay, okay. You're right, Sprinkles. You helped, too. You can have pie tomorrow as well, and we'll take a selfie with you right now."

Molly and I bent down so that our heads were at the level of Sprinkles' head, and Molly took a selfie of the three of us. With our three heads in the frame, there wasn't much room to show the police in the background, but that was okay. The most important thing for the picture to show was that we were together, we were safe, and we were happy. Our detective work had paid off once again.

Chapter Twenty-Three

I headed to the pie shop extra early the next morning so that I had time to bake an assortment of pies for my celebration with Molly and Theo that night. The last few months had been a whirlwind, and I felt like I hadn't really taken time to slow down and celebrate. Tonight, I was determined to change that.

After closing, I pushed a few of the café tables together and set up a smorgasbord of pies. There were far too many pies for them to all be eaten that night, but that was okay. Leftover pie was never a bad thing. I'd made strawberry moonshine pie, peach brandy cobbler, apple bourbon crumble, and death by chocolate pie.

In addition to all the pies, I opened a bottle of pinot noir from Sunshine Springs winery. I had plenty more bottles I could open if we went through that one, and I had a feeling we might.

Molly arrived first. She once again hadn't had time to work with me at the café today due to her job at the library, but I was glad she'd at least been able to get off early enough to come celebrate with us. I was exhausted from working all day without her, but that exhaustion faded away when I saw her smiling face.

"Izzy! What is this? You baked enough pies for twenty people!"

"You're exaggerating. Not *that* many people. But it is a lot. I just wanted to make sure we had options, and that everyone got the pie they love. We all deserve it."

"That we do," a male voice said from behind Molly, and I looked up to see Mitch. He'd snuck in the door behind Molly before it had even closed completely.

I raised an eyebrow at him. "Who invited you to the pie party?"

"Theo. He told me there was a celebration tonight for those who had worked on the Edgar Bates case. I figured my invite must have gotten lost in the mail since I definitely worked on that case." He wiggled an eyebrow at me.

I laughed. "I wasn't trying to exclude you. I just didn't think you'd be interested in hanging out with me after I once again ignored your advice not to play detective."

"It's not advice. It's an order."

I laughed again. "You can't boss me around. Besides, you know you appreciate my help. I've got a knack for solving murders, it seems."

"I hate to admit it, but you do. I'd offer to hire you on the police force, but I already tried that once. Apparently, you think baking pie is more exciting than becoming an official detective."

"It's not that I think it's more exciting. It's that I think I already have enough excitement in my life. Baking boozy pies is just the right level of adrenaline rush for me."

Before Mitch could answer, the bell above my door jingled and Theo arrived.

"Sorry I'm late. I got caught up talking to one of my employees about how we're going to fix that grapevine Peter smashed." Theo shook his head. "I'm just glad we caught him before he did any more damage."

"Don't worry," I said. "You didn't miss anything. Molly and Mitch just got here, too. Mitch tells me you invited him as your date?"

Theo roared with laughter. "What's the matter? Jealous?" He winked at me and I rolled my eyes at him.

"Enough flirting, you two," Molly said. "Let's dig into this pie."

"I'm not going to argue with that," I said with a grin. "Have a seat everyone, and I'll pour some glasses of wine."

A few minutes later, we each had a full glass of wine. We held our glasses high, and Theo led the toast.

"Here's to good friends and good detective work," he said. "Cheers!"

"Cheers!" we all echoed as we clinked our glasses. As everyone started loading their plates with generous slices of pie, I looked over at Mitch.

"So, since I'm sharing my pie with you, are you going to share with me what ended up happening with Peter last night?"

"Sure. It's practically public knowledge by now, anyway. Scott was at the station earlier and heard it all, so I'm sure the gossip train is chugging right along. You'll find out sooner or later whether I tell you or not. Peter gave a full confession, and we found a gun at his house that matched the type of gun that was used to kill Edgar. You were right. He was worried that the speech was going to reveal a secret that would ruin his business. I can't believe that he killed his father over it, but he has always been a bit of a slime ball." Mitch shook his head. "I can't imagine how anyone could be demented enough to take a life, let alone the life of their own father."

"So, Tabitha and Belinda were both completely innocent?" Molly asked.

Mitch nodded. "Yes, they were both innocent—of murder, at least. Tabitha is in a bit of trouble for trying to take stuff from Edgar's house that didn't belong to her. But my guess is that she'll cooperate with us to give it all back, and then try to get out of Sunshine Springs as quickly as she can. There aren't any more old, rich men for her to go after here."

"Theo's rich," I said with a grin. "And old."

Theo glared at me. "I'm only a few years older than you, Izzy."

I shrugged and laughed. "If you're not old, then why so defensive?"

Mitch and Molly laughed too, while Theo's face turned red with annoyance.

"Anyway," Mitch said. "Theo might be old, but he's not old enough for Tabitha. She wants someone who's literally at death's door so that she can quickly claim his fortune as her own. My guess is we won't be seeing her around here anymore."

"And Belinda?" I asked.

"Belinda isn't in any trouble," Mitch said. "At least, not from me. She'll have to figure out on her own how to work out things with Frank, but she didn't break any laws. She intended to break in and steal the speech from the safe, but you guys chased her off before she could actually commit any crimes. The speech did talk about how she was cheating on Frank, but I'm not going to be the one to tell him that. That's on her. She'd better hurry and tell him, though. Word's getting around town. If she hasn't told him already, he'll find out soon enough."

"Was there anything else in the speech about Peter?" Theo asked. "Or was it just the tidbit that he didn't really go to Harvard?"

"The only thing about Peter in that speech was the fact that he hadn't gone to Harvard," Mitch said. "But that was enough. Nobody in Sunshine Springs has ever really liked Peter, and no one really liked doing business with him. We only tolerated him because we thought he was Harvard-educated, and who were we to question his abilities? But if there's one thing folks in Sunshine Springs hate, it's being lied to. Peter knew that once everyone found out that he'd lied about going to Harvard, his business would be as good as done. He couldn't stand that fact, and that's why he shot his dad."

I shook my head sadly. "Poor old Edgar probably never imagined that his son would shoot him to try to keep that secret safe."

"Probably not," Mitch agreed. "I have to say that I'm glad old Edgar left everything to the city. Obviously, neither Tabitha nor Peter deserved any of his fortune."

We all sat and thought about that for a moment as we munched our pie. Then I looked at Mitch and asked, "What else was in that speech? Any more shocking secrets?"

Mitch smiled. "Oh, there were a few shockers. The speech was mostly things I already knew, but there were definitely a few things that surprised even me."

There were a few beats of silence as Mitch continued to eat his pie, and finally Molly couldn't stand it any longer.

"Secrets such as?" she prodded.

"Nice try," Mitch said with a shake of his head. "I'm not telling."

"That's not fair," I protested. "We helped you find that speech. You shouldn't keep all the secrets for yourself."

Mitch's face turned serious. "Listen, I know I like to give you a hard time about playing detective too much. But I promise that I'm not just trying to punish you for always ignoring me and going around sleuthing. I've been a sheriff for a while, and I've seen quite a few things. If there's one thing I've learned, it's that the secrets of Sunshine Springs aren't mine to share. If a secret needs to come out, it eventually will. It's not my job to decide what people should and should not be forced to reveal about themselves. I'm just here to keep the peace, and to eat pie."

With a wink, he shoved another bite of peach brandy cobbler into his mouth.

I sighed. He was probably right, and even if he wasn't, he'd just made it clear that he wasn't sharing. I shrugged, and took a huge bite of my pie as well.

A knocking at the café's front door startled me. I looked up and saw Grams standing there with Sprinkles. She'd watched him for the day so that he wouldn't be stuck in the back room while I was working. I hadn't expected her back quite so soon, but I was glad to see her. Her hair was now electric purple. As I let her in, I laughed to see that Sprinkles toenails were painted electric purple as well. He also wore a bright purple bandanna around his neck.

"Looks like you two had a spa day today," I observed.

"Of course," Grams said. "We spent the whole day at Sophia's Snips. I had to keep up on the gossip. I hear you caught another murderer, Izzy." She reached up and patted my cheek. "I'm so proud of you. You're becoming quite the detective."

Mitch cleared his throat, and Grams moved over to pat him on the back.

"Don't be so grumpy, Sheriff," she said. "You know you love Izzy's help. And don't worry. I'm proud of you, too."

She pinched his cheek, and he rolled his eyes. But then he scooted his chair over a bit to make room for her to sit at the table next to him.

"Here, Agnes. Have some pie."

"Don't mind if I do," Grams said. Within moments she was chowing down on a slice of strawberry moonshine pie. Sprinkles sat next to her, knowing that Grams was his best bet for having bits of pie sneaked to him. Just as I was sitting down again, Scott appeared at the front door.

He pushed on it and found that it was still unlocked, since I hadn't dead bolted it again after letting Grams in.

"Sorry to show up so late," he said as he walked in holding a big box. "I had a package for you, but I couldn't get by until just now. I'm glad to see you're still here."

Mitch snorted. "You couldn't get by earlier because you've been spending so much time gossiping today."

Scott didn't even try to deny that. "Can you blame me? This is one of the best gossip days we've had in Sunshine Springs for a long time. Not only is there a lot of buzz about Peter confessing to killing his father, but Belinda also confessed to Frank that she'd been cheating on him."

I looked up with interest. "She did? I hadn't heard that yet."

"Oh yes," Grams said between bites of pie. "That was all the rage at Sophia's today. Everyone was talking about how Belinda and Frank are breaking up."

I felt a little sad. I shouldn't have been surprised that they were breaking up, but part of me had hoped that somehow they would work it out. Despite my own divorce, and despite seeing so many relationships go sour over the years, there was still a part of me that somehow believed in true love. I still wanted to believe in love stories that conquered the odds, but Frank and Belinda weren't going to be one of those love stories.

"It sounds like Frank actually handled it pretty well," Scott said. "Word around town is that he was heartbroken, but that he had known for a while that the relationship was all but over. And Alice is happy that she got her employee back. Belinda needs money now, and since she doesn't have to sneak around with her new boyfriend, she promised Alice she'll be a lot more dependable at the Morning Brew Café. Alice didn't take a lot of convincing. She desperately needs an employee."

I groaned. "I understand. I still need to hire someone. It's okay now that tourist season is slowing down a bit, but I could still use the help. Especially since Molly is so busy now that the library is about to have a bunch of money."

"Yeah," Molly said. "I almost can't believe it. It's been so long since we've had any significant cash come into the library. There's going to be a lot of work to do revamping things, but I'm excited. And don't worry, Izzy. Even though I won't be able to help out as much, I'm sure you'll find someone. It's only a matter of time until you find the right employee."

I wasn't so sure that she was right, but I wasn't going to worry about it at this exact moment. This was a moment to be happy and to eat good pie with good friends. I invited Scott to join us at the table, and he didn't need to be asked twice. But just as he'd started digging into his slice of pie, the door to the café opened once again. I looked up in surprise, wondering who else could possibly be coming.

To my utter shock, it was Frank. I was surprised he was even showing his face in town on a day like today. He must have known that his relationship with Belinda was hot gossip.

He looked a bit taken aback by the fact that so many of us were sitting there eating pie. "I'm sorry, Izzy," he stammered out. "I didn't mean to interrupt. I just wanted to talk to you about the pie I ordered."

My heart went out to him as I remembered the anniversary pie he'd ordered for Belinda. It was still on my calendar to make, but I assumed he wouldn't want it now.

"It's okay, Frank. I can cancel that order, no problem. I haven't even started it yet, so you won't be charged anything."

"Actually," Frank said, his cheeks turning a bit red. "I was wondering if I could still have the pie, but perhaps without the writing on it?"

"Sure," I said in surprise. "I'd be happy to bake the pie for you and leave the writing off. Do you still want the key lime flavor?"

He nodded. "I like that flavor a lot, and I think I deserve to celebrate life. I'm sad right now, but I'm happy for a new beginning."

I smiled at him. "Trust me, I understand. And there's no better way to begin again than with good pie. In fact, why don't you sit and eat some pie with us right now? There's plenty to go around, and I promise we don't bite."

For a moment, I thought he was going to refuse me. I guess I couldn't have blamed him. I'm sure he knew that we'd been gossiping about him today along with everyone else. But we hadn't been saying anything malicious. I did truly hope that he would find joy in his new beginning, and I was happy when he finally nodded and sat down.

"Okay," he said. "I've been meaning to try some of these pies, anyway. Everyone raves about them."

"With good reason," Theo said around a bite of pie. "I promise you that you've never tasted pie this good."

It only took one bite for Frank to agree with Theo.

"You're right," Frank said around a big mouthful of death by chocolate pie. "That's the best pie I've ever tasted." He turned to look at me. "I'll be sure to tell everyone I work with that they have to come to the Drunken Pie Café and try this pie."

I grinned. "Thanks. I'm happy that everyone's been talking up my pie shop. But all this talking only reinforces the fact that I really, *really* need to find an employee to help me out here."

144

"You're looking for someone to work with you at the café?" Frank asked.

I nodded. "I've been searching for a full-time employee to help out, but it's not easy to find someone."

"I might know someone," Frank said.

I perked up. "Really?"

Frank nodded. "I heard a gal the next town over talking about how she wanted to get some experience in a café, but all the cafés in that town didn't have openings. She might be interested. If you want, I can give her your contact info."

"Yes, please!" I said. "I'd love to talk to her."

Molly grinned at me. "See? Everything is working out just the way it's supposed to."

"Indeed," Grams said. "Frank is happy for a new beginning, the library has plenty of money, Peter is getting what he deserves, and now you're getting an employee, Izzy."

"I hope I am, anyway," I said.

"It sounds promising," Grams said. "Who knows? Maybe once your new employee starts, you'll have some extra time and you can do even more sleuthing."

She winked at Mitch, who only groaned.

"Is it bad if I say that I hope that girl already found a job so that Izzy stays busy by herself here at the pie shop?" he asked.

We all laughed.

"I can't help it if I'm a good detective," I huffed.

Mitch frowned. "And I can't help it if I worry about you when you go chasing after murderers. But, I do have to admit that I appreciate the help you gave on this case." He raised his wineglass. "Here's to Izzy, and here's to hoping that there won't be a need any time soon for her to do more detective work."

We all said cheers and clinked our glasses, and I grinned over at Mitch.

I wasn't going to go looking for more detective work, but if a case dropped into my lap, I wasn't going to refuse it. I was surprised at how much fun sleuthing had turned out to be.

In the meantime, I would enjoy pie and wine with friends. I deserved this celebration, as did everyone at that table.

Everything was right in Sunshine Springs once again.

About the Author

Diana DuMont lives and writes in Northern California. When she's not reading or dreaming up her latest mystery plot, she can usually be found hiking in the nearby redwood forests.

You can connect with Diana at www.dianadumont.com

Happy reading, and happy sleuthing!

Made in the USA
Middletown, DE
03 September 2019